Kisses Worth Waiting For

A FOUND FAMILY ROCK ROMANCE

ELLE WHITTAKER

LEMONADE
HEART
PRESS

Content Guide

This book contains:

Adult language/profanity, people confidently owning their desire, and consensual open-door sex scenes.

Memories of bullying (mild)

Contents

QUEEN ANNE

MARLOWE WAINSCOATE
Guitar, backup vocals. Blue eyes, brown hair. Dating
Simon.

JEM REED
Lead vocals. Militaristic, and known for her killer
performances and full sleeve tattoos. Half red, half blonde
mullet.

ROSE DEVANGELO
Bass. Quiet and caring. Level-headed, short brown
pixie cut.

DUCKY ROBERTS
Drums. Chaotic and funny. Purple hair and lots of
piercings.

THE BOY SCOUTS OF ATLANTIS

SIMON BOROUGHS
Guitar, lead vocals. Rule follower. Dating Marlowe.

WENDY JONES
Drums. Victorian changeling boy who turns feral on the
drums.

FELIX CHRISTOPOLOUS
Keys. Emo kid. Grumpy black cat in both energy and
appearance.

AARON TRUVEAU
Bass. Golden retriever himbo. All-American blonde Clark
Kent, a little gullible.

QUEENSCOUT

MARLOWE, JEM
Vocals

ROSE, AARON
Bass

DUCKY
Percussion

WENDY
Drums

SIMON
Vocals, guitar

FELIX
Keys

"Creep" by Radiohead
"I Want You to Want Me" by Cheap Trick
"It's Friday I'm in Love" by The Cure
"I Believe in a Thing Called Love" by The Darkness
"Here You Come Again" by Dolly Parton
"Can't Help Falling In Love" by Elvis Presley
"Lady" by the Little River Band
"The Wish" by Mindy Gledhill
"But Not For Me" by Ella Fitzgerald
"My Hands Are Shaking" by Sondre Lerche
"Vienna" by Billy Joel
"Kiss Me" by Tom Waits
"At Last" by Etta James

And a woman I used to know
Who loved one man from her youth,
Against the strength of the fates
Fighting in somber pride,
Never spoke of this thing,
But hearing his name by chance,
A light would pass over her face.

SARA TEASDALE
"THOSE WHO LOVE"

Prologue

SOPHOMORE YEAR OF HIGH SCHOOL, AGE 15

ROSE

Click.

The black-haired boy I'd followed to the tech booth frowned down at the door handle. "Oh. Uh," he said. He looked up at me, his eyes a shocking green. It made my stomach swoop.

I'd noticed him the second I'd walked into the classroom. Baggy black jeans, a black and white striped undershirt, the long sleeves poking out from under a black t-shirt. Converse All-Stars. A series of faded concert wristbands on his arms. His hair was longer, hanging in black strands around his face. He was deeply, devastatingly, impossibly cool.

"Don't freak out," he said. "But I think we're accidentally locked in here."

I swallowed. "Do you have your phone?" I asked.

He shook his head. "Do you?"

I shook my head. "It's back in the classroom," I answered. We both looked at the black rolling door that covered the windows to the auditorium. That was locked in place too.

The boy slid down the door and sat, leaning against it. "Whatever. Someone will come find us eventually." He gazed up at me from his spot on the floor. "What was your name again?"

"Rose."

He nodded. "Felix. You're new?"

It was my turn to nod. "I just moved here. From Sacramento."

Felix nodded.

Silence filled the tiny room. It was around the size of my bedroom, but all of the equipment made it feel even smaller. A sound board, a light board, a few monitors. File cabinets were labeled for headsets, microphones, and other gear.

I didn't expect to spend my second day at a new school locked in a tech booth with a cute boy I'd just met. It felt like something from someone else's life—someone daring and fun. Like an accidental game of "Seven Minutes In Heaven." I had no idea if my fellow 15-year-olds still played games like that. Either way, I never had. I'd never even been kissed.

Felix's voice knocked me out of my thoughts. "Why'd you sign up for tech theatre?" he asked.

"Oh," I said. "I…um, I really love music?" I said. I immediately felt idiotic. That wasn't an answer at all. But Felix just looked up at me, patient. I noticed smudged black eyeliner around his eyes. "I'm also in band," I continued. "But I like the tech side of theatre things. With music, I mean. Like…"

I fumbled, trying to find a way to say what I meant,

without rambling even more than I already had. "It's like, music can add so much to a story," I finally said. "In a play, a song can change the mood. I like that."

I expected Felix to make fun of me, but he just nodded, then rested his arms on his knees, interlacing his fingers. I caught a glimpse of black nail polish. "What kind of music do you like?"

It was a little disorienting, standing in the middle of all this attention. "My music taste is kind of…old school and…emo?"

Felix lowered his eyebrows at me and then gestured to his outfit. "Yeah, so am I," he said.

"Yeah, but you're like…cool," I replied.

My statement hung in the air for a moment before he gave me a shocked frown.

"I am definitely not cool," Felix said. "What bands do you listen to?"

I was still kind of processing what Felix had said about not being cool, which is exactly what a cool person would say, but I answered. "AFI. Arms Like Roses. My Chemical Romance. Radiohead. Dashboard Confessional. And this isn't emo at all, but I've been really into The Strokes lately."

"The Strokes are fucking awesome," Felix said.

"Yeah," I replied, smiling. "Fucking…awesome." I hardly ever swore, and the word felt strange in my mouth. "What about you? What bands do you like?"

"I like almost everything. All of the ones you listed," he said. "I'm an insufferable music nerd. Talking Heads. Velvet Underground. Sex Pistols. Lauren Hill. Crass. Siouxse and the Banshees. Billy Joel."

I didn't know if I believed in love at first sight, but maybe I believed in love at first listen. I swallowed. "I love Billy Joel."

Felix grinned suddenly, and it lit up his whole face. I realized I had never seen him smile until this moment. "Billy Joel is the reason I stayed in piano lessons as a kid," he said. "And Jerry Lee Lewis." He thought for a moment, then added, "And Fats Domino. And Tom Waits." He looked up at me. "You can sit down."

"Right." I sank to the floor, kneeling and smoothing my skirt over my tights. I looked up to see Felix gazing at me. "What?"

"You could have taken a chair."

"Oh." He was absolutely right. But it hadn't even occurred to me to sit in a chair. "I was just…"

Felix waved me off. "What do you think of West Oakland High so far?"

I thought. "I haven't experienced very much of it yet," I answered honestly.

"General vibes," Felix said, leaning his head back against the door as he looked at me. "Hallways easy to navigate? General political leanings aligning with yours? Cafeteria layout good?"

"I haven't been in the cafeteria yet," I said.

"Where do you eat lunch?"

I toyed with the hem of my skirt. "The library," I said quietly. It was like, the fourth time I'd felt embarrassed in the last ten minutes. Or maybe there was just a constant undercurrent of embarrassment, and I kept experiencing spikes. Because of course I ate lunch in the library. I didn't know anyone. I didn't even need to visit the cafeteria to know I wouldn't be able to find a place.

And it wasn't just because I was new. I didn't have a place at my old school either. The one girl I'd been friends with since elementary school had moved away before we started high school. I spent my entire freshman year in Sacramento eating lunch in the library. I had just started to make friends with some of the kids in band when I moved here.

But Felix just nodded. "I eat in the library when the weather's shitty. Or if I don't want to deal with people."

I looked up at him. When I first saw him in the drama classroom, I had this idea in my head of some kind of heroic teenage rebel. I thought he probably smoked cigarettes behind the gym and rode a motorcycle. A James Dean type. Jess from Gilmore Girls. Too cool for school, and way too cool to be friends with me. But the real Felix was turning out to be, I don't know, different. More open, somehow.

"You can eat with me and the other tech kids if you want," Felix said. "We usually hang out on the back stairs, by the music room."

Warmth filled my chest. "Thanks," I said. It was such a small thing, but my whole body was reacting like he was handing me a cozy blanket and candy hearts and an adorable puppy.

I started to ask him how long he'd been doing tech theatre, when the door to the tech booth swung open, causing Felix to fall backwards.

"There you are!" Mrs. Tadema said. "What happened?"

Felix slowly got to his feet. "Door locked." He held out his hand to me to help me up, and I took it. His skin was warm and unfamiliar. I felt my cheeks grow hot at his touch. I let go of his hand as soon as I was on my feet. I was waiting for the rest of the class to point and laugh at us for getting locked in together, but everyone else was talking amongst themselves throughout the auditorium.

"We're heading back to the classroom," Mrs. Tadema said. We followed her down one of the aisles.

"Hey, can Rose and I do sound for *The Secret Garden*?"

Felix asked. I looked at him, but all of his attention was on Mrs. Tadema.

"Fill out the form when we get back to class," she said.

Felix and I did end up doing sound for *The Secret Garden*, and Mrs. Tadema trusted me to add underscoring to some of the scenes where there wasn't any, and Felix had the idea of adding nature sound effects. I started eating lunch with him and the other tech kids, and then suddenly, for the first time in my life, I had a small group of friends. Not just one friend. But a group of them. Including Felix.

By our junior year, I was holding in a lot of things that I couldn't bring myself to confess to Felix. But one day, sitting on the back steps by the music room, I would manage to confess that when I said he was cool, I meant that he was cool to me.

CHAPTER 1

"I'll Do It"

ROSE

"I couldn't even like, adjust my mouth to the kiss size," Simon said, his arm around Marlowe. "She was like… it was like she was going to the dentist. Like, AAAAHHH-HH." Ducky collapsed on the floor in laughter, her purple hair covering her face.

Marlowe grinned at her boyfriend. "I think you might win the Most Awkward First Kiss award."

"I don't even know if you can count it as a kiss," Simon said. His hazel eyes danced while he played with Marlowe's long brown hair. "It was a…mouth mauling."

"My first kiss was sweet," Marlowe said, leaning into Simon. "The most tiny, chaste peck after a school dance. I've gotten better at kissing since then."

"Yeah, you have," Simon grinned.

Ducky sat up. "Will you two stop being adorable? Okay. Rose's turn. Tell us your first kiss story."

My cheeks grew hot. I turned back to the cactus plants near the window I was watering, trying to decide if I

7

wanted to make something up to spare myself the embarrassment, or just be honest. The honesty route was painful, but I didn't think I'd be capable of coming up with a good enough lie.

"I um…" I murmured.

"Come on," Marlowe said. "It can't be that bad."

I turned to see four pairs of eyes staring at me. Simon and Marlowe from the couch, Ducky from the floor, Felix from the armchair that had become "his" after the last year of coming over.

"I've never been kissed," I mumbled. Barely loud enough to be heard.

"What?" Ducky asked.

"I said I've never been kissed!" I yelled.

The room was silent.

"No, I heard what you said, I'm just surprised," Ducky said.

"Never?" Marlowe asked.

I put down the watering can and shook my head.

"This is a very personal question, but are you ace?" Ducky asked. "Like, asexual?"

I thought of the yearnings I'd felt for years, the dreams I'd had, both literal and metaphorical. The ache I felt between my legs when I watched a certain boy at the keyboard. "I don't think so," I replied.

Ducky studied my face. "So do you *want* to be kissed?"

"Of course I want to be kissed!" I exclaimed. I was still embarrassed, but Ducky's questions were opening something up in me. "I'm twenty-four years old! I've wanted to be kissed for like, a decade! Longer!"

Another beat of silence. I slumped into a chair.

"I mean," Marlowe said. "I don't blame you. Kissing is awesome."

"I highly recommend it," Simon added, pressing his lips to Marlowe's cheekbone.

Ducky rolled her eyes, "Oh my god, we know. You're into each other."

My stomach rolled. I wasn't jealous of Marlowe exactly. I had zero feelings for Simon outside of friendship. He was like a big brother to me. I just wanted what she had.

But with someone else.

I was very happy for Marlowe and Simon, truly. But my loneliness had grown heavier over the past year. There was so much joy in our house now, even more than there was before, with Simon and the other boys coming over all the time. I was grateful. But my patient heart ached sometimes.

Ducky's voice snapped me back to the present. "I'm asking you this like, practically," she said. "Not just desire-wise. Do you want to be kissed?"

I blinked at her. "What do you mean?"

"I mean that if you want to be kissed, then let's get you kissed!"

"But…how?" I asked.

Ducky shrugged. "We've got tons of options. Tinder, a groupie at a show…"

"Don't be a bad influence," Marlowe said.

Ducky glared at her. "Are you slut-shaming me?"

Marlowe pressed her lips into a thin line and looked thoughtful. "Actually, I think maybe I was? Sorry. That was shitty."

Simon gathered her up into his arms. "My accountability queen!"

"You're forgiven," Ducky said. She turned her attention back to me. "I'm obviously not going to do anything without your consent. But I'm just saying, if you want to be kissed, I will absolutely help make that happen."

"I'd feel weird," I said. "If it was a stranger. It doesn't have to be like a 'Disney true love kiss,' but I don't think I could just kiss anyone."

Ducky nodded. "It needs to be someone you know."

"I'll do it."

My eyes snapped to Felix. He was sitting in his usual chair, in his usual all-black attire. He didn't even look up as he spoke—he was scrolling his phone. When the room went quiet, he looked up at all of us. Even after all these years, there were still startling moments when his green eyes sent electricity through me. When his features took me by surprise.

I could hardly breathe.

Ducky broke the silence. "That…might actually be perfect?"

"What? How?" Marlowe asked.

"Because," Ducky replied. "They've known each other forever, and he's a boy and she's a girl and they're both straight and they're good friends and there are no stakes because there aren't feelings involved."

I swallowed hard.

Simon sat up on the couch. "Wait a minute, what about the Oregon Rule?"

Felix looked thoughtful for a long moment. I could see him weighing the pros and cons, and I couldn't quite breathe. Finally, he said, "It's not like Rose and I would start dating. It's just a kiss."

My blood was on fire. For so many reasons. Because Felix was talking about kissing me. Because he was saying we *wouldn't* start dating. Because *the boy I'd loved since high school was talking about kissing me*.

Marlowe leaned forward. "Wait, but we're all literally

in a band together now. All the Boy Scouts of Atlantis and all of Queen Anne. So Oregon Rule still applies."

Ducky leaned back, resting on her hands. "Yeah, but the Oregon Rule is 'no dating or hooking up with people in the same band or a band you're on tour with.' It doesn't say anything about 'a friend kissing another friend as a favor.'"

Felix stood and stretched. I glanced away from the thin strip of skin I could see when his t-shirt lifted. "Exactly." He looked over at me, and I felt my skin flush. He searched my face. "But if you don't want to, that's fine. I'm just offering as a friend. I'm going home. Are you coming?"

I sat frozen. For the last year, as Felix had gotten into the habit of coming over, I'd gotten into the habit of walking him home. Those ten minute walks were precious to me, but now this one felt loaded. Anything could happen on a walk. And everyone in the room knew it.

I debated with myself for a moment. I didn't want to lose our walks, now or ever, because of some kind of awkwardness. But I didn't want to deal with everyone else's awkwardness if I stayed here. Finally, I nodded and stood, feeling faint. I was grateful that Marlowe, Ducky, and Simon didn't make a big deal out of my walking home with Felix, after the conversation we had all just had.

I felt unsteady on my feet as Felix and I walked the few blocks to the apartment he shared with his bandmates. His offer to kiss me was ping pong-ing through my whole body. I couldn't think about anything else. But Felix was his usual serious self.

When we got to his place, he stopped on the sidewalk.

We never stopped on the sidewalk.

"Rose," Felix said. I lifted my gaze to his.

"Yeah?"

"Are you okay?"

I nodded. "Yeah," I said. "Just…yes."

"I didn't mean to make things weird," Felix said.

"You didn't!" I exclaimed. Even though he most certainly did. But I didn't want him to feel bad about it. "*I'm* just weird. It's me. Like, you didn't make things weird, they were just weird to begin with. Because I'm weird."

Any other boy might have tried to contradict me, but Felix just shrugged. "The offer still stands," he said. "If you just want to try kissing with someone with no stakes or whatever. Just to get it out of the way."

I could kiss Felix. He could kiss me. It could even happen right now, here on this cracked sidewalk, if I wanted it to. After years of trying to shove down every daydream I'd ever had about it, it could actually happen.

Kind of.

It was like being told I could hold a star, but only for a second. Unwrapping a Christmas present that was meant for someone else. It would be a shadow of what I actually wanted.

But if I could never have the real thing, maybe a shadow would be enough.

I swallowed. "Can I think about it?"

"Sure," Felix said. "I'm not worried about fucking up our friendship either way."

"Yeah," I said.

"Don't look so freaked out," Felix said, a hint of a smile in his voice. "It would just be a kiss. It's not like we're in love or anything."

"Right," I said.

Then I watched him walk into his apartment and close the door.

The Ledge

By Rose Devangelo

He is the most hopeful ledge
I've ever stepped near.
I wonder if his soul
would still recognize mine
if the title I greeted him with
changed.
I can imagine
jumping off that ledge
and growing wings on my way down.
I can imagine
looking back up
and seeing his face
looking down at me,
his feet steady on the ground.

CHAPTER 2

I Don't Believe in a Thing Called Love

FELIX

There was never enough room for everyone's instruments. Forming a band with eight members was the stupidest idea any of us have ever had. We didn't *need* two bassists. I kept trying to convince Rose and Aaron to trade off, but apparently that was a dumb suggestion. And Ducky on percussion plus Wendy on drums was insane. But Queen Anne and the Boy Scouts of Atlantis had had so much fun playing that dumb trees song we'd written on tour together, that we decided to form a super-band called "Queenscout." And now somehow, stupidly, we were recording an album?

We were all crowded into the garage behind our apartment building, because it was the only place with enough room, but that was being generous. We had to run extension cords from outside, and I was convinced we'd blow a breaker one of these days. I was shoved into a corner behind my keyboard, which was annoying because I literally couldn't leave unless like four other people moved out

14

of the way, and everyone who had a guitar of any kind had to be careful when they turned so that they didn't hit anyone.

Jem raised her hand and all of us stopped playing. "Let's try slowing the bridge down," she said. When Jem wasn't head banging with her half-blonde, half-red mullet, she ran band practice with an iron fist. Other people might be more diplomatic with their suggestions, but I liked that Jem just got to the point with it.

"Like, half time?" Aaron asked, adjusting the strap on his bass.

"Like da, da, da, da, dum," Jem replied, clapping to demonstrate the rhythm.

"Ooh ooh ooh! Wendy, hit each beat on the bass drum?" Ducky said.

Wendy tossed his hair away from his face and looked into the air for a second, working out the pattern.

"Go from the end of the last verse," Jem said. "From 'dipping it old school.' Two, three, four!"

We launched into the middle of "French Fry Milkshake," and Jem was absolutely right—the bridge was way better when we slowed it down.

I glanced over at Rose, who grinned at Aaron as they created two layered bass lines, Aaron plodding up and down slowly while Rose filled in with something more melodic. She had swept part of her wavy, short brown hair up into a clip of some kind. I couldn't remember if I'd ever seen her hair like that. It looked nice.

Cute, actually? She looked…pretty.

It had been three days since I'd offered to kiss her, and she hadn't mentioned it since. It was a genuine casual offer, purely a favor to a friend. So I couldn't really figure out why I kept thinking about it. Or why Rose had gone radio silent about it. We'd been friends for a decade, and Rose is one of like, four people on the planet who has ever seen me cry, so I didn't think our friendship was in danger. It just felt weird that we hadn't talked about the kiss offer again.

Jem's voice knocked me out of my thoughts. "Felix, solo to finish the song, go!"

I moved my fingers up and down the keys, riffing on the chords, improvising a solo. When we'd gone through the verse once, Jem gave the signal for our chaotic, cymbal crashing finish. Half of us laughed out loud with satisfaction when the music ended.

Jem clapped. "Okay, five minute break, everyone." She and Simon and Marlowe made their way to the apartment while the rest of us stood around.

"Damn, Felix," Ducky said. "Panties will be flying through the air if you play like that at the next show."

"As long as it's not hearts," Wendy teased.

Aaron furrowed his Clark Kent brow. "Hearts flying through the air sounds super gross, actually."

"It was a metaphor," Wendy replied.

"I don't want hearts," I said. "Metaphorical or literal."

"Felix swore off love five years ago," Rose said. I glanced up at her, and she gave me a warm smile, her soft brown eyes affectionate. I knew she was teasing, just like Wendy was, but she was right.

"Exactly," I said.

The only serious relationship I'd ever had was in college, and it had ended in total disaster. It had blown up my life *and* the band I was in, and honestly it was just proof of what I'd known since I was a kid. That rejection was always a possibility and that it sucked ass when it (inevitably) happened. It sucked so bad that it wasn't even worth it to get into a relationship.

Ducky's voice reverberated through the room. "Do you

not believe in love at all? Or do you believe in it and just think it's not for you?"

"Why are you speaking into the mic right now?" I frowned.

"For emphasis," Ducky replied, her words amplified. She lowered her voice an octave, for further emphasis, probably. "Answer the question."

I shrugged. "Both?" I said. "I don't know if love exists, but if it does, it's probably not for me."

I caught Rose's eye, and for some reason, she blushed. And there it was again, the thought that had leapt into my mind earlier. That Rose looked pretty.

What the hell?

Maybe it was because I had said something about kissing her. Because now that I thought about it, had her lips always looked that full and soft? What would it feel like to take her face in my hands, to tangle my fingers into her short wavy hair?

"What about sex?" Ducky asked, shaking me back into the room.

"What about it?" I asked.

"Do you believe in sex?"

"Ducky," Rose admonished.

"It's a valid question!"

"As an outside observer," Wendy said, glancing up from his moleskin notebook, "It seems like Felix does believe in sex." I swear I never knew when that guy was paying attention. He was either being insane on the drums or he was like, communing with spirits or some shit. I still wasn't sure if Wendy was totally human.

Aaron was tuning one of his bass strings. "Like that it exists or that it's for him?"

"Both," Wendy said.

Suddenly everyone in the room was looking at me. "I believe in sex," I said.

Which was true. I just didn't believe in love. Casual hookups? Sign me up. Friends with benefits? I'm golden. Catching feelings? I would literally rather walk into the ocean with rocks in my shoes.

"Did you just say you believe in sex?" Simon asked, stepping back into the garage.

"That should be a track on the album," Marlowe added.

Jem strode over to her place at the mic again. "Only if it connects to the road trip theme."

"People have sex on road trips all the time!" Marlowe replied.

As the two of them argued, my eyes wandered over to Rose again. She was smiling that soft, quiet smile of hers— the one she often had in moments like this, when all of us were at band practice together, or talking in a greenroom, or having a big group dinner. She had always been able to sort of "blend in" better than I could, but we'd both always been weirdos. I just broadcast my outsider status more obviously, with my black eyeliner and nail polish and chains. Rose had like, librarian vibes. But I knew she'd struggled to find belonging, too. And I knew how she felt, when she smiled like that. It was kind of miraculous, having a whole group of friends like this, who all made music together. It took us both a long time to find it, and I knew she treasured it as much as I did.

We almost lost it all, a year ago. When Simon and Marlowe had gotten together, they'd done it in secret, breaking the "Oregon Rule" we had in place to keep things as drama-free as possible. It took a while for all of us to get over it. It brought some shit up for all of us, but probably me most of all. I'm the one who made the "Oregon Rule," almost entirely because of that miserable college breakup.

Honeslty, I still thought the rule made sense. If Simon and Marlowe ever broke up, we were all fucked.

When I tuned back into the conversation in the room, Marlowe and Jem had reached an agreement that a song about believing in sex could be on the album, as long as the sex was specifically roadside motel sex and the lyrics weren't too explicit.

"I'm on it," Simon grinned. "Give me like, two weeks."

"We're supposed to start recording in a month," I said. "So if it sucks, we're not putting it on the album."

"What about the ancient mariner song?" Jem asked me.

"What about it?"

"Is it done?"

I waved dismissively. "I'll have it next practice."

"I'll start writing the roadside motel one tonight," Simon replied. "And if it sucks, I won't show it to you guys."

"Fine." I took a swig of my water bottle. "I say we title the song 'Roadside Motel.'"

"I second the motion," Rose said, raising her hand.

Her smile went right through me, leaving a faint buzzing behind.

CHAPTER 3

Alameda Beach

ROSE

My body hummed from the eye contact with Felix as we started jamming on another song. Actually, my whole body had been humming for the past three days. I kept hearing Felix's voice in my head, casually offering to kiss me.

"I'll do it."

"I'll do it."

"I'll do it."

And I hadn't been able to decide what I actually wanted. I wanted Felix to kiss me, desperately, but I didn't know if I wanted it like that. A friendly "ripping off the band-aid so that I could say I'd been kissed" kind of kiss.

But I also didn't know if I would ever have another opportunity to kiss Felix in my life. He literally just reminded everyone in band practice that he didn't believe in love or dating or any of it. I'd already broken my heart so many times over Felix, wanting him, waiting for him. So maybe a kiss between friends would be the best that I could expect.

Maybe it was worth breaking my heart one more time for.

I glanced over at Felix, frowning in concentration while his hands moved over the keyboard. I did a walking bass line to echo what he was doing on the piano, and he looked over at me and nodded in time to the music we were making together. Felix had that look on his face, the one he only had when he was playing music—present and alive and bright. It was like he actually glowed, despite all the black he always wore.

He smiled at me.

And in that moment, I knew. Yes, I wanted him to kiss me. Yes. Yes. Yes. Whether tonight or tomorrow or next week, the answer was yes.

And I'd better say something soon or I'd lose my nerve. After band practice, I took my time packing my gear and putting it in Jem's car. Felix was covering his keyboard when I walked up to him.

"Can I talk to you?"

I thought I saw something pass over Felix's face—a split second of unexpected openness. "Alameda Beach?" he asked.

I nodded.

Alameda beach is barely a beach, but it has sand and gently lapping waves and we'd been going there since we were teenagers. We walked the four blocks from the boys' apartment in silence, then sat down in the sand.

I stared out across the bay. The San Francisco skyline was visible a little to the north, lights turning on as the sun set. I glanced over at Felix, his features still as he looked across the water.

I didn't think I'd have the courage to say it if I was

looking at him, so I stared down into the sand instead. My heart was pounding so hard I could almost hear it. My words came stumbling and rushing out.

"I've been thinking, and I um. I want you to kiss me."

Silence stretched out for several seconds before I could bring myself to look over at Felix. His eyebrows were raised, but he was giving me a half smile.

"Yeah?" he said.

"Yeah," I replied, slightly breathless. "I think? No, yes."

"Yes?"

"Yes." I looked into Felix's eyes, and I was suddenly flooded with certainty. "Yes."

"Once or more than once?"

My stomach swooped. "I didn't know 'more than once' was an option," I managed.

Felix looked over the water thoughtfully. "I guess I'm asking if you want to just be kissed or if you want like, an ongoing education. Like, practice."

I swallowed. The idea of "practice kissing" was too unexpected to even comprehend. I didn't even know it was an option.

"Is that allowed? Under the Oregon Rule?" I finally managed. I knew the deep reasons why Felix had made the rule all those years ago—the heartache it came from. The idea of an "ongoing education" with Felix was making it hard to think straight, but if Felix was going to bend the rules, I needed to know he was on solid ground about it. Because I certainly wasn't.

Felix took a breath. "As long as it's a short-term thing, I think it's fine."

I nodded.

"Do I have to decide right now?" I asked.

"Nah, you can decide about the ongoing thing later."

I nodded, lifting a handful of sand and letting it fall

through my fingers. Both my request and Felix's offer hung in the air between us, electric, buzzing.

"Do you want me to kiss you right now?" he asked.

There had already been a whole roller coaster zipping through me, but Felix's words sent my insides into yet another loop. Answering him felt like jumping off a cliff, but I had to grab this chance with both hands before it was too late. "Yes, please."

Felix stood, then held his hand out. "Come here," he said.

"Do we have to be standing?"

"Not necessarily," Felix shrugged. "It's just easier."

I reached out and let him haul me up. He didn't let go of my hand. For a moment, we just looked at each other.

It was me who broke the silence. "I'm nervous," I said, honestly.

"Why are you nervous?"

"I don't know. What if I'm bad at it?"

I watched Felix's eyes drop to my lips. "I doubt you'll be bad at it."

He took a step closer to me, and I felt my breath quicken. He reached one hand out and gently cupped my face. And then Felix's eyes moved over my features—my eyes, my lips.

I couldn't think. I couldn't breathe. I could just stand there, looking at him looking at me.

And then he leaned in.

And then Felix Christopolous, the boy I'd loved since I was sixteen years old, pressed his lips to mine.

His mouth was gentle. He tasted like chapstick and summer and music. My bones seemed to sing with his touch. Without making a conscious decision to do it, my lips molded to his. Felix brought his other arm around my waist and pulled me closer to him. I felt myself gasp slightly.

Felix's lips parted slowly, experimentally, then closed against mine again, moving tenderly.

I had never felt anything so wonderful in my life.

Both of my arms moved up to circle his body, my blood singing, my head spinning. Felix parted his lips again, and I clutched handfuls of his jacket, certain I would fall over if I didn't hold on to something. When his mouth finally left mine, I simply stood there, eyes closed, swaying.

"Hey," Felix said gently. I finally opened my eyes to find him gazing at me.

"How do you feel?" he asked.

"Like…like I'm on the moon," I grinned, breathless.

Felix gave me one of his rare, blinding smiles. He was still holding me, one arm firmly around my lower back, the other hand cupping my jaw. He leaned in and kissed me one more time, a short, tender peck, then released me and took a step back.

"Is it always like that?" I managed.

Felix chuckled, another rare phenomenon. "Not always. But I can confidently say that you are not bad at kissing, Rose Devangelo."

I was going to pass out. I sat down on the sand with a thump. One brief, hysterical giggle escaped me. I couldn't believe that had just happened. The fact that I had just kissed someone was insane enough, and the fact that the person I had just kissed was *Felix Christopolous* didn't even seem real. And kissing him had felt so incredible I didn't even know how to process it.

"Are you okay?" Felix asked.

I looked up at him, standing above me. "Yeah," I said. I felt jittery and hopeful and alive. Felix sat down beside me again, and I looked over at him. The joy buzzing in me made me bold. "Can I kiss you again?"

Felix smiled again, more gently this time. His tender gaze was intoxicating. He leaned into me, bringing his face close to mine, and I closed the distance between us.

This time, when Felix parted his lips, I felt his tongue lick gently into my mouth. That was all it took for the sensations in my body to ratchet up to eleven. Or, like, eight hundred. I was suddenly ravenous for him. I wanted to touch all of him at once. I had an insane urge to crawl into his lap.

I shifted so that I could face him better, my tongue moving against his. I had no idea what I was doing, but the pleasure of it made me confident. I could taste the cool metal of Felix's lip ring, could feel his warm hands move up my arms, then tangle into my hair. After a little while (I had no idea how long), I stopped and leaned my forehead against his, trying to get my heart rate down to normal. With my eyes closed, I smiled.

"If kissing is this awesome, what is sex even like?" I joked quietly.

"We can do that, too, if you want," Felix said. I could have sworn he sounded a little breathless.

My eyes flew open. I pulled away and stared at him.

"Not like, right this second, obviously," he clarified.

"Right." I couldn't get my brain to function. I felt foggy, either because of kissing Felix or Felix offering to have sex with me. Both of those things could have been responsible for my inability to form a single thought.

Felix frowned and leaned back a little. "Shit, was that not…? Sorry, was that out of line?"

I shook my head, probably a little too vigorously. "No, no, that was completely in line, I just…I was just surprised. Is all."

Felix shifted so that there was a little more distance between us. I watched him bite a fingernail and stare out over the water, looking troubled.

"Really," I said. I reached out to lay a hand on his knee. "I wasn't offended."

He turned to me and his face softened. In the years that we'd been friends, I'd never gotten to see this side of him. He was so gentle and open that I felt dizzy with it. We'd been vulnerable with each other in other ways in the past. But this was something more. Like I'd discovered a door in a house and opened it to find an entirely new room.

"It's a standing offer," Felix said. "Ongoing education in general, or practice, or whatever. In kissing, or sex, or whatever you want."

I nodded. "I'm too…overwhelmed? To think clearly. About any of that. But I'll let you know."

Felix nodded back, and then both of us turned to look out over the water. After a few seconds, I rested my head on his shoulder. We watched the lights of the San Francisco skyline until he hauled us to our feet to walk home. I couldn't stop smiling the whole time.

CHAPTER 4

You're the Only One Drinking

FRESHMAN YEAR OF COLLEGE, AGE 18

ROSE

"Are these shoes good with this outfit?"

My roommate Xalia stood in my doorway, sporting wedge sandals and a black sundress. "They're cute, but you might get uncomfortable standing for a long time," I replied.

"You're right. You're always so right." Xalia paused. "You can borrow my red skirt if you want."

I glanced down at my outfit, a t-shirt and overall shorts. "Do I need to borrow your red skirt?"

Xalia shrugged. "No, you look fine. Just like, if you wanted to get flirty tonight, you could wear my red skirt."

I went back to my task of lacing up my Converses. "I don't know how to flirt," I replied.

"I told you it's a learned skill!" Xalia said, stepping out of her shoes and walking to her bedroom.

"I think I'm just bad at romance."

Xalia returned, boots in hand. "Rose, you're like, the most lovable person I know."

"I don't think I'm unlovable," I clarified. "I just don't know how to make romance happen."

"Well, if ever you want a wing woman, I've got you."

My phone dinged. "Felix is downstairs," I said, and we met him in the parking lot to walk to the show together.

When we got to the venue, Felix frowned up at it. "This is where the show is?"

"It's the address on the poster," Xalia replied. "And there are people inside."

"What the fuck is this place?" he grumbled, stepping forward.

I look up at the blank space above the storefront. "I think it used to be a Payless shoe store?" I replied.

I kind of loved this about college. That my friends and I could go to a rock show in an old Payless shoe store. Last week, we went and saw a band play in an abandoned granary. Felix always found these weird underground shows, and it made me feel like I was part of something rebellious and beautiful. As we stepped inside the Payless, I could feel the bass pulsing from the first band. I watched the crowd jumping around in the shifting lights, and smiled. The room was about two hundred degrees and it was perfect.

When I glanced over at Felix, he was biting his lip in this really attractive way, his tongue fiddling with the lip ring he'd just gotten a few months ago. It startled me, sometimes—how attractive he was. I'd seen his face almost every day for the last two and a half years, but every now and then, the light caught his profile in a certain way, or he'd look at me with his green eyes, and I'd fall for him all over again.

I'd almost come to accept that he would probably

never love me the way I loved him. I had tried to stop hoping. But my stubborn heart kept beating for him, anyway. So I'd just gotten used to loving his friendship for what it was and trying not to ache for more.

That was probably the reason I was "bad at romance." Because I didn't really want it with anyone unless it was Felix. I'd probably been subconsciously self-sabotaging, just in case Felix looked at me one day and thought, "Yes. It's been Rose all along." I didn't want to be unavailable if that were to ever happen.

I watched Felix step into the crowd, and Xalia grabbed my hand and yanked me along with her. "Come on!" she shouted. I knew both of them were going to squeeze their way through the crowd to the mosh pit. I usually stayed on the outskirts, watching everyone shoving and throwing their bodies around. It was often a little too rough for me, but there was something beautiful about it. The affectionate violence of it.

The band was good. They played fast and hard and loud. I watched the bassist's fingers as he played. I played upright bass in high school, and right after graduation, I'd gotten an electric bass guitar and an amp. I wasn't amazing, but I was having fun learning. Maybe I'd be able to play in a rock band someday. That was the dream.

Four songs later, the heat was getting to me, so I tapped Xalia's arm. "I'm going outside for a minute!" I shouted. She nodded and went back to dancing. I didn't actually know how she or Felix could survive moving around like that in this small, hot room. I was having fun, but I was also dying for a bit of air.

I stepped out onto the sidewalk, where a handful of people were standing around, smoking. I sat down on a bench a little away from the crowd, letting the breeze run over my skin.

"Oh, hey, Rose," a voice said.

I looked up. Mal, a guy I sat next to in English class was smiling down at me, a beer in one hand.

"Hi, Mal," I replied, smiling. I wouldn't exactly call us friends, but we were friendly in class.

"Is this seat taken?" he asked, gesturing toward my bench. I could hear a slight slur in his voice.

I shook my head and he collapsed onto the bench next to me. "Killer show," he said.

Now that he was closer, I could see the thin sheen of sweat on his forehead, curling the hair around his hears. The sickly sweet smell of beer wafted toward me.

"Yeah," I replied.

Mal turned and looked thoughtfully at me. "Listen," he finally said. "Sorry if this is weird, but I've been thinking it all semester. You're really beautiful, Rose."

I felt a little ping of surprise. The compliment seemed genuine, despite the alcohol on Mal's breath.

"Thanks," I said.

He held out his bottle in offering, but I shook my head. He took another swig and leaned back on the bench. He glanced over at me again. "Damn, maybe I shouldn't have said that. Although, whatever, shoot your shot. Do you want to go out sometime?"

I suddenly realized that I had never in my entire life been asked on a date like this. *Did* I want to go out with this guy from my English class? I opened my mouth to ask him for more details, but he held a hand up to cut me off.

"No, wait. Don't answer. I'm too drunk to remember."

I bit back a smile. This whole situation was feeling more and more ridiculous. Although maybe when he was sober, it would be fine to go out with him. He wasn't... unattractive. Maybe we could go to dinner and see a movie or something? That's what people did on dates, right?

I glanced at the door of the venue and thought of Felix inside, his eyes closed, throwing his body around to the music. Maybe I should just live a little. Go on a few dates with this guy from my English class. I turned back to Mal to find him still looking at me.

"Maybe I should just kiss you," he slurred.

All of my thoughts screeched to a halt. I'd pictured my first kiss in dozens of ways, but none of them were this. None of them were a drunk guy from my English class, slurring on a bench outside of a rock show at an old Payless Shoesource.

But then again…maybe this was as good as it was going to get for me. I felt my unkissed status like a ball and chain, getting heavier as time wore on. To go through high school without kissing anyone was okay, but college was when you were supposed to have fun. When you were supposed to make bad decisions with strangers. (Or semi-okay decisions with friends from class.) And if I were to let Mal kiss me right now, it would at least make a great story later.

True. I didn't feel any specific desire to kiss the guy on the bench next to me. But another part of me felt like maybe I should just get it over with. I took a deep breath.

"You can kiss me," I said.

Mal's eyes were a little unfocused on my face. He leaned in, and I steeled myself for whatever was about to happen.

But then Mal stopped and leaned away again. "No," he said sadly. "I shouldn't take advantage. Not when we're drinking."

"You're the only one drinking," I pointed out. But he raised his hand to cut me off again.

"I gotta go. I can't make decisions when we're drunk. See you in class." And then Mal stood and stumbled away, taking a last swig of his beer, which was definitely not his first.

At least he was trying to be a gentleman. I guess?

I sat outside for a few more minutes, then made my way back inside to the show, still unkissed, and still pining for my best friend, who was currently jumping up and down to the music.

I'd write a poem about it all later. I'd write dozens of them.

CHAPTER 5

Aqua Tofana

FELIX

"Could I get more bass in my monitor?" Wendy called out.

Tori, the sound guy, made an adjustment while Rose and Aaron both plucked out a bass line. Wendy nodded and grinned. "Thanks!" he yelled.

We played through the last verse of the song, and then Tori gave us a thumb's up. With sound check out of the way, I stepped out from behind the keyboard. "So I've been thinking," I said. "And I don't think Simon should sing lead on Aqua Tofana."

"Why not?" Simon frowned.

"Because it's the most fucking feminist song we have, and with an even number of guys and girls in this band, it makes more sense to have a woman sing lead."

"Hey," Ducky said. "That's a good point! Why the hell is Simon singing lead on that song?"

Jem looked thoughtful, her blonde and red hair swept into two ponytails. "Who should sing melody?"

"Um, you, duh," Ducky replied.

"Okay, then who's singing harmony?"

"I can do it!" Marlowe said. "I mean, if it's okay with Simon."

"I can sit out that song completely if you want," Simon said.

"No, you should still sing on it," Ducky said. "Because men can be feminist, too. But you just shouldn't sing *lead* on it."

"That's fair," Simon replied.

Marlowe walked over and threw her arms around him. "Ugh, my feminist boyfriend!" He leaned over to kiss her.

Ducky rolled her eyes at them, and for some reason, my gaze went to Rose. She gave me a good-natured smile.

An unfamiliar warmth moved through me, and my mind was suddenly flooded with memories from the beach two nights ago. Rose's soft full lips, the tiny hungry noises she made when I kissed her. The way her body felt against mine.

Don't be a creep, I told myself. *Rose just wants some experience, and you got distracted because kissing feels good.*

If I was being totally honest with myself, I'd been thinking about those kisses with Rose more than I thought I would. Damned if I knew why. She hadn't said anything about my offer of sex, but I knew I'd better get ahold of myself if that was what she wanted. I didn't want to destroy eight years of friendship just because I was getting weird about things.

Wendy's voice interrupted my thoughts. "I'm going next door for Thai food, if anyone wants to come."

I glanced at the time. "We've gotta be back by eight," I said.

The next few minutes passed in friendly chaos, with everyone putting gear in cases and arguing about Thai food. All eight of us ended up at the Thai place, so we took over one of the long tables near the window. I had a vision of getting a bunch of entrees and splitting them, and spent five minutes trying to organize everyone's food preferences before giving up and letting everyone fend for themselves.

Wrangling eight band members stressed me the hell out. Thank god for Jem, honestly. We were kind of co-leaders by now.

You'd think that Jem and I would be closer, since we're both band leaders. But we hadn't really bonded very deeply. I appreciated her leadership for sure, but we weren't like, best friends or whatever. Jem was actually probably closest with Rose out of all of us.

Even though Jem was intense, onstage and off, Rose was like, the least intense person I knew. But I looked down the table to see their heads bent together, talking quietly. They'd been close from the moment they'd met, even though they were complete opposites. I saw Rose smile at something Jem said, and another flutter passed through my chest.

Maybe Rose and I's friendship was unexpected, too. I'm this anarchist emo kid with a lip ring and Rose is the shy girl next door. She's so sweet all of the time, and I know I come off as surly to just about everyone. But Rose was just…she was so easy to talk to, from the first moment I met her, and something about her friendship sort of kept my hands on the wheel. I didn't really know what I would do without her.

Aaron took a bite of his chicken satay and turned to me. "Do you have a set list for tonight or are we winging it?"

I looked down the table at Jem, still deep in conversation with Rose.

"Eh, we'll wing it," I said. "Let's at least do Aqua

Tofana, French Fry Milkshake, and Uh Oh CEO. And whatever Jem says."

"Sweet," Aaron replied.

I WOULD NEVER EVER EVER GET sick of playing shows. When I was a tiny kid, I hated sitting at the piano. My mom made me do scales ten times before I could get up and I loathed every second of it. She was always pulling out simplified Beethoven songs for me to learn. But around age nine, I discovered rock music, and the piano came alive for me. Jerry Lee Lewis and Fiona Apple and Tom Waits all made their way under my skin, and suddenly the piano became a place where I could put everything I didn't have words for.

It was still that way for me. Even if the music didn't match how I was feeling, it still did something just to play it. Even on a song like "Aqua Tofana," which was feminist in a way that I had no personal experience with, I could feel the music rearranging me inside, putting things to rights.

I looked up at Jem, screaming into the microphone. I was absolutely right about her taking over vocals on this song. She brought a rage and power to it that Simon just didn't have.

We were getting to the climax of the song. Everyone else cut out, and Wendy and I locked into a rhythm together, starting small and building. Then Rose added a bass line, then Aaron echoed it, adding to the build. Simon and Marlowe both came in on guitar for a few bars, then I did a run down the keys until the song exploded into the final chorus.

Fuck, it felt good.

The crowd was screaming and jumping around, and I couldn't help grinning. We landed the final chords of the song and I looked over to see Rose laughing out loud with the joy of it.

We made eye contact while the crowd cheered, and she gave me a happy look, her face covered with a thin glow of sweat from the lights. She looked so pretty.

I returned her smile and then looked back down at the keys, pretending to adjust some settings. *You know where these kinds of feelings end*, I thought. *Cool it.*

We usually saved "Aqua Tofana" for last, but we had like ten more minutes to play, so we did a new one called "Hieroglyph," which in my opinion, was not ready, but it went okay. We finished off with the OG trees song, the one we wrote when we first went on tour together last year. I didn't think I'd ever get tired of how it felt to have a crowd of people cheering for something I helped make.

You could always clearly tell the introverts from the extroverts in Queenscout by how everyone acted after a show. Aaron, Ducky, Marlowe, and Simon all stood around and talked with people for way too long, while Rose, Wendy, Jem, and I packed up our gear, and then usually our extroverted bandmates' gear. If ever the extroverts got mad at us for how we handled their stuff, that was on them.

I lowered Simon's guitar into its case and snapped it shut.

"You were right about 'Aqua Tofana,'" Rose said. I looked up to see her wrapping a cable nearby. She smiled at me.

"I know," I replied.

"It was a good call. Thanks for saying something."

I shrugged. "It's a better song with just the women singing."

"And more feminist," Rose said, a teasing edge in her voice.

"And more feminist," I repeated, pulling gaff tape off the carpeted stage. I paused, then added, "I felt like a dick for suggesting it."

"Why?"

"Because a guy making a suggestion about a feminist song feels dick-ish."

"That just proves you're an actual feminist," Rose said. I could still hear the smile in her voice.

"Whatever," I grumbled.

I glanced up at Rose, who had picked up another cable and was wrapping it carefully. That was something I always appreciated about Rose. How she did things carefully. Or, not quite carefully? More like…deliberately. Intentionally. Rose took her time with whatever task she was doing, giving it her full attention.

She kissed that way, too.

I wondered if she would give other activities the same present, quiet attention—activities that went beyond kissing. If she would be all steady hands and eye contact and—

Shut it down, asshole, I said to myself. *Don't get ahead of yourself.*

If Rose wanted more, I'd be happy to help. As a friend. No need to get carried away.

CHAPTER 6

The Journalism Details

ROSE

Jem frowned down at the mixing bowl in front of her. "This is the most unhygienic thing we've ever done," she said.

"And also the most brilliant," Marlowe replied. "Everyone get a spoon!" She was placing half a dozen maraschino cherries on the top of what was definitely the largest ice cream sundae in history. Or at least in the history of our home.

Jem opened one of the kitchen drawers. "How did this even start?"

"We were out of clean bowls," Ducky explained. "So I started putting ice cream in the mixing bowl just for myself, and then Marlowe wanted some, and then the communal ice cream sundae was born."

"'Communal ice cream sundae' is a super gross phrase," Jem said. But she dug her spoon into the ice cream anyway.

I took a spoon and scooped out a bite. "We should

make this a tradition," I said. I tried to sound as casual as possible as I added, "Invite the boys over for the next one. Sunday Night Sundae."

"That's such a good idea!" Marlowe said.

Ducky elbowed her. "You and Simon can have cherry stem tying contests."

"That sounds like a euphemism," I laughed.

"We could all compete!" Marlowe replied. "Measure all of our kissing skills!" Then she caught my eye and her face dropped slightly. "Except Rose? I guess. Maybe this is a bad idea."

And then I couldn't help it, I felt my cheeks burn. I absolutely hated blushing. Why oh why did it have to happen?! What evolutionary purpose did it serve to advertise to the whole world that I was embarrassed about something? I wished I could just hide my embarrassment, but instead my whole face was turning red.

"Wait," Ducky said, looking hard at me. "Wait. Rose. Holy shit. HOLY SHIT!"

I dropped my spoon and covered my face with my hands, but I'm sure my grin was still visible.

"You got kissed?!" Marlowe exclaimed. She practically threw her spoon onto the counter. "Felix?"

I peeked at her through my fingers and nodded.

Ducky hopped onto the kitchen counter. "Oh my god, Rose, tell us!"

I dropped my hands. I couldn't stop smiling. "It was… good?" I said.

It was perfect. It was a dream come true. It was a hundred thousand wishes and hopes distilled into a single lovely night and I know I sound like a lovesick teenage girl but I haven't been the same since.

Is what I didn't say.

Marlowe swatted my arm. "Come on! Give us details!"

I saw Jem glance at me and then the others. "She doesn't have to tell if she doesn't want to."

"Come on!" Ducky cried. "Sharing first kiss stories is a time-honored feminine tradition!"

"I don't know what to say," I replied.

Marlowe took another bite of ice cream. "When did it happen? Start there."

"Five days ago?"

"'*Five days ago*'?!" Marlowe exclaimed. Her blue eyes widened at me. "This happened five whole days ago and you didn't *say* anything?!"

"What should I have said?" I asked.

"I don't know," Ducky replied. "How about 'hey guys, I had my first kiss'?"

"Hey guys, I had my first kiss. Felix kissed me," I said. I felt my smile practically take over my face as I said it out loud. I realized I hadn't said it out loud until that moment. My blood fizzed.

"Okay, give us the journalism details," Marlowe said. "Who, what, when, where, why, how."

"Felix," I said, trying to control my grin. "Kissing. Five days ago, after band practice. On Alameda beach. Because I asked him to. And um…well."

"Well what?" Jem asked.

"That's how he kissed," I replied, feeling my cheeks heat again. "He kissed well. I mean…not that I have anything to compare it to. But it was…enjoyable."

"So did you kiss or did you *kiss*?" Ducky asked.

I tried to steady myself with another bite of ice cream. "I think both?"

Ducky grinned. "What a fun first kiss story!" she said. "It's unusual but kind of fun."

Something in me fell a little. I hadn't really thought about that. Did Felix's lips on mine even count as a first kiss? If it was just a favor from a friend? Maybe a "first kiss" was more than just lips touching—maybe there had to be actual romantic feeling behind it for it to count. Years from now, when someone asked me about my first kiss, would this be the story I told? The one of a friend from high school kissing me on Alameda beach because I was twenty-four and inexperienced? Or would I have some other story to tell, some truly romantic moment under the stars?

Those moments with Felix had felt romantic. And they were under the stars.

"Tongue?" Ducky asked.

Before I could answer, Jem interrupted. "Okay, reminder that you don't have to share details, Rose. You can just say you plead the fifth."

Thank god for Jem.

"I plead the fifth," I said.

"That's right. Way to live in alignment with your value of self-worth," Jem replied. I smiled at her. She probably would have been fine with me sharing details if I had wanted to, but she knew I had a hard time saying no when people asked me things, so she gave me an out whenever she could.

Marlowe took another bite of ice cream. "Are we allowed to ask 'what now'?"

I stalled by scraping the side of the mixing bowl with my spoon. "Yes," I said. "But I actually don't really know the answer."

"Let's start with the Oregon Rule," Marlowe said. Her words were weighted, and I could understand why. Last year, she and Simon broke the Oregon Rule by secretly getting together without anyone else knowing. We'd all healed from that betrayal, and Marlowe and Simon were great together. But I think the memory of that pain was still fresh.

"Well, the Oregon Rule is about dating and hooking up," I said slowly. "Felix would just be giving me…education."

Everyone's eyebrows went up at once.

"Wait, is this an ongoing thing?" Marlowe asked.

"It…could be?" I replied. "We haven't talked about details yet. He just…offered."

"Are you telling us," Ducky said, "that Felix offered you kissing lessons?"

"He did," I said. My heart beat a little faster in my chest at the memory of it.

Ducky grinned. "Dayyyyum," she said. "That's kind of hot."

You have no idea, I thought.

Marlowe poured another tablespoon of chocolate syrup over the remaining ice cream. "And is that what you want?" she asked. "Kissing lessons?"

Yes. Yes, dear god, yes. I want to kiss Felix Christopolous every single day for the rest of my life.

"Maybe," I shrugged. When I looked up everyone was watching me closely. "I mean…I really enjoyed kissing, and I'd like to get better at it. If that's a thing. And I'd like to…" I felt my cheeks heat yet again. "I'd like to experience other things. Too."

Jem set her spoon down. When I looked at her, she was gazing thoughtfully into the distance. "Honestly, a friends with benefits situation is the best way to get your first time out of the way. That's what I did and I have no regrets."

"What?" I exclaimed. First of all, was Jem giving her blessing to this thing with Felix? And also how did I not know this about one of my best friends?!

Marlowe nodded. "I mean, everyone's first time is

usually awkward and messy and dumb, so it would almost be easier if there was no actual relationship at stake."

"I mean, Felix and I have a relationship," I countered.

"But not a romantic one," Marlowe replied.

Ouch. My stomach clenched at Marlowe's observation. But I couldn't argue with it.

"Okay, but if you do decide to do it," Ducky said, "use lube. Like, more than you think you need."

"And wear a condom," Jem said.

"Obviously," I replied, even though I hadn't actually put that much thought into either of those things. My daydreams (and sometimes actual dreams) didn't really have that much detail. I liked to think I would have thought of them in the moment. Or maybe Felix would?

"And pee afterward," Marlowe said. "And maybe stretch your hip flexors if things last for a while."

"And you can put a towel down on the bed if you're worried about the lube making a mess," Ducky added. "Or like, anything else making a mess."

I suddenly realized that I might not have any actual idea what I was doing.

Sex education in California was famously more comprehensive than in other states. But I couldn't remember if peeing afterward was ever part of the curriculum. Lube might have been, but probably not a towel. Would I really need a towel?

And what was like, the etiquette of sex? Who was in charge of condoms? I decided to ask at least that much.

"Who's in charge of bringing the condoms?"

Ducky and Marlowe answered in unison.

"The girl," Ducky said.

"The guy," Marlowe said.

They frowned at each other. Jem leaned in. "Everyone should bring condoms, just in case. If he brings some, you don't have to worry about it. And if he doesn't, you have some."

"Got it," I said.

Ducky must have sensed I was feeling overwhelmed, because she gave me a warm smile. "Whatever you decide to do," she said. "We've got you."

"We can even take you to buy condoms and lube," Marlowe added.

"Girls trip to the sex shop!" Ducky yelled, lifting her spoon into the air.

I laughed. The idea felt absurd, but I suddenly saw the appeal of having the guidance of these friends. "I'm in. Even if I don't sleep with Felix, I want to be prepared for when I sleep with *someone*."

CHAPTER 7

No Details Needed

FELIX

"Fuck, sorry, guys," I said, shaking my head. I'd just messed up the bridge of "Double White Lines" for the third time in a row. I was having trouble focusing. I'd been having trouble focusing for like, a week.

Which was bad news. Because the thing that was breaking my focus was a constant background hum of thoughts about Rose.

Rose, who was my *friend*. Nothing more.

I mean, not *all* of my thoughts were kissing thoughts.

How had we known each other for so long without me not knowing that she'd never been kissed? (Until a week ago.) Why hadn't it ever occurred to me that she didn't really seem to date? And actually, why didn't she ever confide in me about guys at all?

She'd been there to listen to me talk about Eva, the one relationship I'd had in college. And I didn't talk to *anyone* else about it. I think one of the reasons Rose and I were such good friends was because we're both kind of private people.

But realizing that Rose had never talked to me about a crush or anything kind of stung. I'd been thinking about that for the last week, too.

I stretched my hands out in front of me and cracked my knuckles.

"Let's go from the second verse," I said.

This time I played through the song perfectly. During the last verse, I made eye contact with Wendy, who was playing with his usual intensity. That kid was a completely different person behind a drum set. Gentleman (like, literally gentle) in the streets, absolute demon on the drums. He grinned at me. It was enough for me to lock in to the rest of practice. We played through some old tunes and messed around on a new one Simon wrote.

One of the reasons I loved music was because it took up enough space inside of me that there wasn't room for anything else. Whatever else was going on could get knocked aside while I was on the keys. Playing music sort of reset me. By the time I was covering up my keyboard, I was feeling less distracted.

"Hey, whatever happened to the whole kissing Rose thing?" Simon asked.

I grimaced. So much for music being a good reset.

"The whole WHAT?!" Wendy demanded, his eyes wide. I looked over to see him frozen in the act of covering his drums.

Simon closed his guitar case. "We found out that Rose has never been kissed, so Felix offered to kiss her."

Aaron frowned at me. "What happened to the Oregon Rule?"

"Just a friendly favor," Simon explained. "You know, to just get it out of the way."

"I'm more surprised Rose has never been kissed," Wendy said, returning to his task. He looked up at me. "Unless *you* kissed her…?"

I didn't answer. Instead, I adjusted the cover on my keyboard, or at least pretended to.

Aaron leaned against the wall of the garage. "Wait, if she's never been kissed, does that mean she's never—"

"That's none of anyone's business," I snapped. Aaron held his hands up in surrender.

"We're just curious, man," Wendy said. "So…did you kiss her?"

I set my mouth in a firm line and continued to adjust the cover on my keyboard. "If I answer, will you shut up about it?"

Wendy held up three fingers in the boy scout salute. "Scout's honor."

"Yes, I kissed her."

The room was so quiet that I looked up. All three of my bandmates were just looking expectantly at me. "I'm not giving any of you assholes any details about it," I added.

"No details needed," Simon said. He paused. "I just…"

I raised my eyebrows at him.

"I'm just saying that with our history with the Oregon Rule, I don't want anyone keeping secrets," Simon said. "I know it worked out okay with me and Marlowe, but we could have saved everyone a lot of heartache if we'd just been honest."

"What are you asking?" I said.

"Is there something more going on between you and Rose?"

I rolled my eyes. "Don't be dumb."

"I'm not being dumb."

I looked up to see Simon frowning at me. An ache of regret filled my chest. "Sorry, Simon," I said. "Me and Rose are friends. Always have been, always will be. Any more questions?"

"Is this an ongoing thing?" Wendy asked.

I shrugged. I really wanted this conversation to be over. "I offered. She said she'd let me know." The room went silent. "What?"

All three of my bandmates exchanged a look. Then Simon spoke up. "Really throwing the Oregon Rule out the window, huh?"

I frowned at him. "No? I'm not?"

Simon folded his arms. "Oh, really? How? How is this not breaking the Oregon Rule?"

"Because it's not real," I replied. "Because it's temporary. Rose and I aren't *actually* dating. Even if we do more than kiss, it's not like actual romantic feelings are involved. This is a favor for a friend."

Simon kept his arms folded and just looked at me. Aaron was the one who broke the silence. "Can I…? Just don't do something…how do I say this? Don't…? I guess just tell us what's going on. If there's anything to tell. Even if it's just a friends ongoing thing."

I fought the urge to roll my eyes again. "Yeah, I'll be sure to keep you all updated on my sex life." I knew I was being kind of a dick, but I was too annoyed to do anything about it. "I'm going for a walk," I said, then strode out of the garage, not looking back at any of my bandmates.

ALAMEDA BEACH WAS a ten minute walk from our place, and I found myself there without even deciding consciously to go. My thoughts tumbled through my head as I walked along the sand. The more I thought about the conversation that had just happened, the angrier I got. Why the hell did those guys think they had a right to know anything about me and Rose? Or Rose at all? It was none of their business.

Or maybe it was. Since not dating fellow band members was a standard we'd held onto pretty tightly in the past.

But it wasn't like Rose and I were dating! We were just kissing. Or had kissed. I didn't know if we were still kissing because she said she'd get back to me on it and she hadn't.

Why hadn't she, actually? Did she…fuck, did she not like it?

I thought back to a week ago, the two of us on this very beach. She seemed to like it. She'd gone in for more. And the "more" had been good enough that it made me offer to have sex, which I had completely not planned on doing. The words had left my mouth before I had time to think about them, and then as soon as they were out, I didn't regret them.

Because I wouldn't mind having sex with Rose. In fact, maybe I'd…like? Having sex with Rose?

I'd done the "friends with benefits" thing a few times, and it had always been great. No expectations, no hurt feelings when it fizzled out. Hell, I liked those situations more than one night stands most of the time. Wendy once told me that the first five times you have sex with someone didn't count, since you were still learning about each other. I didn't know if I totally agreed, but he did have a point. Things did get better when you got to know someone. Whether they liked it fast or slow, or if they preferred a certain kind of foreplay, or if they disliked their neck being kissed, or whatever.

I wondered if Rose would like her neck being kissed. I

thought of her smooth skin, the softness of it when I'd held her face, right before I kissed her. Would the skin along the side of her throat taste the same as her lips? What about along her collarbones…?

I shook my head. *She hasn't asked you, you lecher*, I thought to myself. For all I knew, Rose had gotten what she needed from me and that was that. We'd go back to being the friends we'd always been, no harm, no foul.

Although it was kind of weird that she hadn't gotten back to me about any of it. I pulled out my phone and glanced at it. No messages.

If I didn't hear back from her about my offer in another week, I'd say something. But not until then. Until then, I'd just be the friend I'd always been to her. And I knew she'd be the same to me. And it was a perfect situation, honestly. Rose and I were such good friends that I didn't think we could mess anything up by having sex, and we didn't have to worry about something dumb like catching feelings.

I sighed. The guys at practice had probably been right to question me about it. I'd been a jerk. I turned around to walk back home and apologize.

And I wouldn't check to see if I'd gotten a text from Rose.

CHAPTER 8

Can I Just Wallow For a Second?

FRESHMAN YEAR OF COLLEGE, AGE 18

ROSE

I glanced down at the screen of my phone. Felix. I felt a pleasant flutter in my chest, but then I frowned. He never called. He always texted.

"Hello?" I answered.

"Rose?" a broken voice said.

My thoughts went static. I had never heard Felix sound like that.

"What is it?" I asked. "Are you okay? Where are you?"

"Can you come over?" Felix asked. There was so much pain in his voice that I wanted to tear my skin off.

"Yes, give me ten minutes," I said. I was on my way to a history class, but I turned right around to head to Felix's apartment.

"Door's unlocked," he said. And then he hung up.

My mind swirled with dread. I couldn't imagine what would make Felix sound so upset. He didn't have much family—it was just his mom. Had something happened to her? I walked faster.

Felix's apartment was quiet when I opened the front door. His roommates must have been in class. I made my way down the hallway and pushed Felix's door open.

He was sitting on the edge of his bed, his head cradled in his hands. He looked up at me with tears in his piercing green eyes, and I felt my heart break with an audible crack.

"Felix," I said. I dropped my backpack and rushed to him. We weren't really the kind of friends who hugged, but I didn't think, I didn't wait, I just sat down next to him and gathered him into my arms.

He clung to me, his head against my shoulder, his arms wrapped so tightly around my body that I could hardly breathe. "Felix," I whispered again.

But he didn't say anything. It was as if he couldn't even talk. I felt one great wracking sob leave his body, and the noise he made broke my heart a second time.

I scooted us up the mattress and leaned against the wall, pulling Felix with me. And then I just let him cry. His tears soaked the shoulder of my sweatshirt, his fingers pressing deep into my flesh as he gripped me. It felt like I was the only thing keeping him from flying into a million pieces.

I was trying not to break into a million pieces myself.

After a while, Felix's sobs quieted, and I tentatively ran a hand through his hair. A hundred emotions were buzzing inside of me. The sorrow of whatever had made Felix cry like this. The absolute rightness of him being in my arms. The longing to be able to hold him like this all the time.

But I could also sense that my feelings weren't exactly the priority right now. I could sort them out later. Right now, Felix was hurting.

"Do you want to talk about it?" I finally whispered.

Felix didn't look up at me when he answered. "The band broke up," he said.

"Oh, Felix," I whispered. For as long as I'd known him, all he'd wanted was to be in a band. When Avonswan played their first show, he came to life onstage in a way I had never seen before.

"And Eva and I broke up."

I tried to steady my breathing. If my emotions were battling each other before, they were in an all out war now. I was absolutely heartbroken that Felix was hurting. And I was absolutely overjoyed that he wasn't with Eva anymore. And I felt absolutely guilty about my joy.

I didn't have anything against Eva necessarily. I didn't really even know her that well. It was just that if Felix was going to be with anyone, I wanted it to be me. He and Eva had started hooking up while their band was on tour in Oregon during Spring Break. It had been less than a month since they'd gotten back, and it had been torture to see them together.

But it was torture to see Felix hurting now.

"I'm really sorry," I managed.

Felix's head was still buried against my shoulder, muffling his voice. "Roger gave me some bullshit about 'stealing his girl,' which didn't make sense because they weren't a thing, he just liked her, which I didn't know about. And then Berric said I was just fucking her to get to her dad."

I frowned in confusion. "To get to her dad?" I repeated.

"Apparently Eva's dad is an executive at some record label," Felix replied. He sat up and wiped his nose on his sleeve. He looked at me pleadingly. "I swear I didn't know."

"I believe you," I said.

Felix lifted his head and then rearranged himself so that he was leaning against the wall next to me. He pulled his knees to his chest. I ached to have him close again, but I settled for having one of his arms pressed against mine.

"What did Eva say?" I asked. "Unless you don't want to talk about it."

"She thought things were casual between us. Apparently." Felix rested his chin on his knees. "At band practice, I called her my girlfriend without thinking about it, and everything just...blew up. I hadn't planned on telling anyone that we were together, but maybe we weren't even really together? She said..." He swallowed hard. "She's been seeing a few other guys."

I ached for him. "I'm so sorry."

Felix sighed shakily. "And now there's no more band and no more Eva and I'm just the same fucking loser I've always been."

"Don't say that," I said. "You're not a loser."

Felix made a grumbling sound. "Can I just wallow for a second?"

"Sorry," I said. He looked up at me and I gave him a small smile. "You can wallow."

Felix straightened his legs out and leaned his head against the wall again. His eyes fell closed. "I'm making a rule," he said. "From now on. No getting involved with anyone I'm in a band with. Or on tour with. I'll call it the...I don't know. The Oregon Rule. Because all of this shit started in Oregon."

"That's probably a good rule," I said. I uttered a silent prayer that Felix and I would never end up in a band together, even though it was all I'd been dreaming about for the last year and a half.

While Felix sat with his eyes closed, I took in his features. His straight, perfect nose. Smudged eyeliner. The small silver lip ring he'd recently gotten. It suited him so well it was almost hard to remember what he looked like without it.

"I think I loved her, Rose."

My throat tightened. I wasn't going to survive this conversation. I couldn't do it. I couldn't bear to listen to him talk about loving another girl. But I was frozen in place—I couldn't move or breathe.

"Or maybe not," Felix said. "I don't know. Maybe love isn't for me."

I managed to take a breath. "All love?" I asked.

Felix stared at the ceiling. "I can love my friends. My mom. My—" he swallowed. "My future band mates, if I ever have any again. But romance is…I don't think I'm built for romance."

"You never know," I said, trying to keep my voice even.

But Felix shook his head. "I fucked up spectacularly," he said.

"None of this was your fault," I said, but Felix didn't seem to hear me.

"I've never fucking known what I was doing when it came to romance. Never. I still don't. But if it leads to feeling like this, it's not goddamn worth it. And if it breaks up a band, then it's not worth it."

I didn't say anything. I didn't trust myself to be able to. Felix turned to me.

"Hey Rose?" he said.

"Yeah?"

"Do you wanna cut class and go get ice cream?"

I smiled at him. "I'm already cutting class."

"Then let's go get some ice cream," Felix said. He scooted to the edge of the bed and stood up, then held a hand out to me. "I'm just going to lean hard into the whole 'wallowing' thing for a second. Embrace my emo nature."

I took his hand and let him haul me up. "You can wallow," I said. "I'll even wallow with you. If you want."

Felix nodded, then glanced at my clothes.

"I got snot all over your sweatshirt," he said. "And eyeliner."

I pulled at the fabric to examine it. He was right. I looked back at him and smiled. "We're friends forever now," I replied.

"I fucking hope so." Felix looked at me for a moment, then pulled me into a hug. I sank into it, the warmth of him, the safety of him. I was still overwhelmed with all of my own feelings, but at least I had this. I would always have Felix. Here. Solid. Some part of his heart belonging to me, even if the rest of him didn't.

Break Through
By Rose Devangelo

Years ago, we
bought two dozen plates from the local thrift store
and spent an evening hurling them
at a cement wall by the railroad tracks,
screaming with the clink and shatter.
We walked away breathing heavy
with release.

And there was that camping trip,
When we launched rocks into the lake,
naming the things that each stone stood for
as they crashed into the rippling water,
until all was still and peace inside us.
I chose my words carefully then.

And I think of my heart,
the crack and splinter
of the past year,
how release requires something
being broken.

I think of the word "break through"
and how I think
the operative word isn't "break"
but "through."

I do not know how to let him go
No matter how much it breaks me.

CHAPTER 9

New Bass Strings

ROSE

"**B**rought new bass strings," Felix said, shutting the front door behind him. I looked up from my place on the couch. A familiar warmth spread through my chest at the sight of Felix, his usual all-black ensemble, his painted nails, his green eyes.

"Thanks," I said.

"Hey, Felix," Jem said from the other couch. Marlowe and Ducky were out somewhere.

"Hey."

I put my book aside. For a moment, I felt uncertain—things still weren't quite the same between us after our kiss, but I didn't want our friendship to get even weirder. I took a breath. "Wanna help me put them on?"

Re-stringing a bass definitely wasn't a two-person job. I just wanted the company. And Felix knew it.

"Sure," Felix said.

I stood and walked down the hall to my bedroom, my

heart pounding. *Just two good friends, heading to my bedroom to re-string a bass*, I thought. *Nothing more.*

Felix flopped onto my bed and opened one of the packages of bass guitar strings. He glanced around, his eyes landing on the shelf below my window. "Did you get another snake plant?"

I smiled. "I'm surprised you noticed," I said.

"Honestly, same," Felix replied. "This place is a fucking jungle."

He was right, but I wouldn't have had it any other way. I loved the ritual of caring for houseplants—watering and re-potting and adjusting who got more sun. I think I had about thirty different plants in my room at the moment, mostly succulents, but there were a few spider plants, pothos, and others.

I picked my bass up from where it was leaning in its stand and brought it over. "I like my jungle," I said. I set my bass on the bed between us and started loosening one of the tuning pegs. After a moment, Felix reached over and started loosening another.

I stole a glance at him. His dark hair fell over his face, looking so familiar that I was certain I could pick him out from a crowd of a hundred people by that specific shade of black alone. He'd been dying it every other month for as long as I'd known him.

We worked quietly, pulling the strings out of the pegs and then out of the bridge. I started to put one of the new strings on, but Felix grabbed my wrist. A jolt of electricity went through me. I looked up at him.

"Do you want to clean the neck at all?" he asked.

"Oh." I replied. "Yeah. Hang on."

I always did that when I replaced the strings on my guitar, but apparently I was distracted today. I grabbed some microfiber towels from the hall closet and ran them under cool water. I almost splashed some on my face too, just to cool myself down. Back in my bedroom, I handed one of the rags to Felix and sat back down across from him.

"You start at one end and I'll start at the other," he said, running the cloth gently over the frets at the top of the neck.

I nodded, and began wiping the frets down near the pickups. I stole another glance at Felix. He was so focused, his green eyes trained on what he was doing, his tongue fiddling with his lip ring. He worked slowly, his strong hands gentle.

I watched as his fingers made sure every inch of the guitar's neck was clean. He lavished each fret with attention, running the damp rag over the polished wood of the fretboard meticulously.

Then his hands stopped.

"Rose?" he said.

I looked up at his face. "Yeah?"

"Were you going to clean your half?"

I realized that I'd been sitting frozen, my rag hanging loosely from my hand. I took in his features—his familiar sculpted nose, his green eyes. His lips.

"Can we kiss again?" I blurted.

I hadn't intended to say it. But Felix was unfazed. He simply leaned over and pressed his lips to mine.

A current of electricity hummed through me. Then Felix pulled away, and I swayed forward as the contact was broken. I opened my eyes to see him moving the rag over the fretboard again.

My voice was small when I spoke again. "Can we kiss more?"

Felix looked up at me, searching my face. My heart seemed to stop for a moment. Then he climbed off my bed. He lifted the bass guitar and placed it gently on the carpet. He closed my bedroom door. Then he came and sat next to me.

Felix cupped my jaw, his fingers curling into the hair behind my ear. For a moment he just looked at me. "Is this you asking for an ongoing education?" he asked.

It was difficult to form a coherent sentence, especially when his thumb started brushing over my cheekbone. But I managed a strangled, "Yes."

"What kind of education?" Felix's voice was soft.

"Kissing," I said. "At least. Maybe more."

"Why?" he asked.

My brain felt fuzzy with Felix so close, his hand caressing my face. But I could tell it was important to answer. "Because…because I want the experience. I want to know what I'm doing. And if I'm learning how to do something, I want to do it with someone I trust. Someone safe."

"You can take your time, Rose," Felix said quietly. "If you want. It doesn't have to be me."

I didn't know if I would survive my next sentence, but I said it anyway. "I want it to be you."

Felix searched my face, and I thought that if *something* didn't happen in the next few seconds, I might accidentally blurt out everything. How I'd loved him for years, how I adored everything about him, how kissing him had been a million dreams come true. How I wanted him to be mine forever even though I was almost certain it wasn't what he wanted. But I couldn't afford to tell him any of that, not now.

I swallowed. "Plus I feel stupid for being a virgin at age twenty-four."

Felix paused, then dropped his hand from my face. He stared at the carpet, and I stared at him. Was he surprised to hear that I was a virgin? He must have known, right? I'd never been kissed before last week—he had to know.

"What's a virgin?" he said, looking up at me.

I blinked at him.

"I'm being rhetorical, but what's a virgin?"

"Someone who's never had sex before," I replied, frowning at him.

"Right," Felix said. "What kind of sex?"

"Um. Intercourse sex?"

"So are all lesbians virgins?" Felix asked.

"Oh," I said. I truly had never thought of that before.

"I'm not trying to be a dick right now," Felix continued. "I'm just…I don't believe in the concept of virginity. What the fuck does it even mean? Like, why are we dividing people into categories based on what they have or haven't done? And assigning worth to those categories? Like women should be 'virgins' and men shouldn't be, when literally none of it actually matters. The whole idea of 'virginity' is stupid patriarchal bullshit that perpetuates colonial heteronormative gender roles."

I stared at him. If Felix didn't kiss me in the next five seconds, I was going to explode. Why was it so hot when he got all philosophical and feminist?!

I spoke in a rush. "I absolutely agree with you about virginity and I want to talk more about it but right now I want us to kiss again please."

Felix smiled at me. He didn't smile quickly or easily, but when he did, it softened his entire face. "Okay, come here," he said. Felix scooted so that he was sitting crosslegged on the bed, and I scooted forward so that our knees were touching.

He took my face in his hands. When our lips met, I felt my whole body leaning toward him. Felix's mouth opened gently against mine, our warm breath mingling.

It was even better than I remembered.

I reached out and clutched handfuls of his shirt, yanking him toward me for more. He fell forward, his hands slapping down onto my thighs to brace himself. I reached my arms up around his neck.

I almost cried when Felix pulled away.

"Hang on, this is dumb," he said.

My stomach sank. But then Felix backed up so that he was sitting against my headboard, his legs stretched out in front of him. "Come here," he said. "Next to me."

I crawled over and started to lean my back against the headboard, by Felix's side, but he put a hand behind my back. "Sit facing the door. Put your legs over my lap."

I moved so that I was sitting next to him, then lifted my legs and draped them over his thighs. One of his arms came around my back, holding me in place. I knew that if I were to lean back, he'd catch me.

"Yeah, this is better," he said. Then he leaned in and kissed me again.

He was right. This was better. I parted my lips to let him in, deepening the kiss. Our tongues tangled, and any worry I had about "doing this right" flew out of my mind. I was moving on pure, delicious instinct.

Felix's lips left mine to press against my jaw, then a spot beneath my jaw. He slowly kissed down along the side of my neck, making my back arch.

"Do you like that?" he whispered into my skin.

"Yes," I managed to gasp.

"I'd been wondering," he murmured.

I was trying to process that statement, but then he kissed his way back up my neck and I stopped being able to think. He lingered when his lips made my breath catch. When his mouth found mine again, I was so hungry for him I could barely control myself.

After a few minutes, Felix's lips made his way down my throat again, his chin just barely brushing the tops of my breasts. And suddenly I wanted way more of him touching me there.

I could barely breathe, but I managed to whisper, "I want…can you…will you…?"

"What?" Felix asked softly, his face still buried against my skin.

Maybe I seriously didn't know what I was doing. How did people ask for anything? I had a vague feeling I was supposed to phrase it in some kind of sexy way, but I had a feeling that talking dirty was still several lessons away, if I even got to that at all.

Felix lifted his head and looked at me. "What do you want me to do?" When I didn't answer, he reached up and cupped my chin. "Just say it. Even if it's awkward. You can just be blunt. It doesn't have to be sexy."

Warmth filled my chest. He knew me so well, better than anyone in the world. Of course he knew I was worried about sounding sexy. I took a deep breath. "Grab my boobs," I said.

Felix's eyebrows raised, but he reached up with his strong hand and cupped one of my breasts. And dear god, it felt so good. My head tipped back, my eyes falling closed. He massaged me gently, then did the same thing to the other one. A rush of heat moved through me, and I tilted my head to kiss him again.

We kissed and kissed and kissed. Touching, feeling, exploring, everything slow and torturously wonderful. My whole body was humming by the time Felix climbed off my bed. I glanced at the clock as he stood and straightened his clothing. More than half an hour had passed.

"Do you have to go?" I asked. I sounded a little out of breath.

"Sorry, Rose," Felix replied. "Band practice."

If he had to stop kissing me, at least it was for something as important as music. "I'll text you," I said.

"Duh," he replied. He leaned down and pecked my lips quickly, then strode out of my room.

I collapsed backward and stared at the ceiling. I was pretty sure that counted as a full on make out session.

I just made out with someone.

I just made out with Felix.

I covered my grin with my pillow.

CHAPTER 10

Sunday Not Fun Day

The day after Rose and I made out in her room, the guys and I all walked to Queen Anne's apartment. They'd invited us over for ice cream, and when we entered the room and got a glimpse of the kitchen table, Wendy's eyes widened. "This is disgusting and I'm so excited about it," he said.

He would be.

"That's the spirit!" Ducky said, bringing over a large glass baking pan—the kind you make casseroles in.

The table was covered in ice cream sundae ingredients. Simon and Aaron had brought our household's contributions earlier today (bananas, whipped cream, sprinkles). Queen Anne had told us they were starting a tradition called "Sunday Sundae," which apparently involved making one giant communal ice cream sundae and eating it. In the glass baking dish Ducky had just brought over.

And I stood there, surrounded by people I cared about, and all I wanted was for all of them to be quiet. I was

68

pissed off about how loud it was, and about the people who left trash on the sidewalk on the way here, and the bicyclists that went too fast outside, and the way everyone kept reaching over each other to grab spoons. All of it annoyed me.

Damned if I knew why.

I made my way to "my" armchair and collapsed into it. Queen Anne's apartment was "open concept," so I could still hear and see everyone freaking out about a giant ice cream sundae a few feet away.

A giant ice cream sundae that everyone shared was stupid. We would all have to agree on all of the ingredients in order for everyone to enjoy it, and then even if we did, it was a total germ fest. I pulled out my phone.

At some point, Aaron yelled over to me. "Felix! Do you want ice cream?"

"Nope," I said, not looking up.

But the longer I sat in my chair while everyone else ate their stupid group ice cream sundae, the more annoyed I was at being left out. Which was extra dumb because I was leaving *myself* out. They literally invited me and I told them no, so why was I so butt-hurt about not being included?

I closed my eyes. What did I actually want right now?

If I was being totally honest, what I really wanted was to make out with Rose in her room again.

Or. No. Maybe?

For someone who had never kissed anyone before, Rose was really good at it. Equal parts softness and enthusiasm. It had felt good to have her legs over my lap, to have her hands in my hair. I glanced up at her, eating ice cream with everyone. There were things about her body that I hadn't really paid much attention to before. The way her short hair curled around her ears. The creamy skin of her thighs. And her boobs were like, exactly the right size. I thought of how perfectly they fit in my hands yesterday. I wanted to touch her again.

Just then, Rose looked over and caught my eye, and I darted my gaze down to my phone again. *Cool, just got caught checking her out*, I thought. Fuck.

A few minutes later, I looked up again to find Rose walking toward me, carrying a small bowl of ice cream and a spoon. She handed it to me with a smile. "You looked left out," she said quietly.

I grumbled a thanks and took a bite. Chocolate ice cream with bananas. Exactly what I would have gotten for myself. Rose settled into the couch nearby. I noticed that she had her own small bowl.

"Shitty day?" Rose asked.

I made a non-committal noise and took another bite of ice cream.

Rose glanced over at the kitchen table, then looked back at me. "Did you talk to the boys about, um, us?"

"They know we kissed." For some reason, my stomach flipped when I said it.

Rose nodded. "Are they okay with us continuing that?"

I shrugged. I hadn't gotten around to telling them that yes, Rose and I were continuing to kiss and possibly were going to do more. "I'll tell them later tonight if you want."

"That would probably be a good idea."

I followed her gaze to the kitchen table, where Jem was lecturing everyone on the proper way to cut bananas.

"It's lengthwise for a banana split!" she yelled. "That's why it's called a 'split'!"

"But it's still a split if you cut it in half short-ways," Wendy retorted. "Plus then you don't have to look at all the seeds."

Aaron looked at him blankly. "Bananas have seeds?"

"They're fruits!" Jem replied. "That's what the little dark brown things in the middle of the banana are."

"Which you don't have to see in detail when you split it in half short ways!" Wendy cried.

"Oh my god," Jem said, shaking her head.

Ducky gave Aaron a long look. "Did you really not know bananas were fruits?"

"I knew they were *fruits*, I just didn't realize they had *seeds*," Aaron replied.

The only people not part of the banana conversation (aside from Rose and me) were Simon and Marlowe. I watched as they both stuck maraschino cherry stems in their mouths for a tongue-tying contest. When Marlowe won, Simon swept her up into his arms, kissing her deeply while her legs dangled toward the floor.

Something like acid churned in my stomach.

Rose's voice broke through the chaos of the room. "How's that new song coming?" she asked. "The ancient mariner one?"

"It's fine," I said. In truth, I hadn't touched that song in weeks, even though I told Queenscout I would have it done by the next practice. Sometimes it was just hard to fucking write.

I didn't realize I'd said the last part out loud until I saw Rose nodding. "I can imagine it's hard to write sometimes. Sometimes the muse is just quiet." She looked thoughtfully at me for a moment before turning her attention back to her ice cream. "Have you ever…you don't have to answer this, but have you ever written about Eva?"

My eyes snapped up to hers. "What made you say that?"

Rose's cheeks colored. "I was just wondering," she said. "It was a big deal when it happened, and sometimes people make art about the big things that happen to them.

Maybe a song or two would be good therapy or something."

Rose and I hadn't really ever talked much about the night that Eva and I broke up. The way I sobbed like a little kid, the way she held me. And I super did not want to talk about Eva right now.

"Not everything has to be art," I said. "Jesus."

She frowned at me, and I could not for the life of me figure out why I was being such a dick.

"I'm going home," I said, standing. "Thanks for the ice cream."

I didn't look back as I made my way to the door.

It was quieter on the street outside, and as I walked, my thoughts quieted a little, too. When I got back my place, I kept walking. I had a feeling I still had to sort a few things out.

It had been more than five years since Eva and I broke up, and when I thought about her now, I truly didn't feel anything for her. No lingering attachment to her as a person.

But the betrayal of our breakup, the emotional wreckage of it—*that* I still carried with me. No matter how many times I tried to exorcise it.

What I didn't tell Rose is that I *had* tried to write songs about it, years ago, right after it all happened. But I couldn't do it. Every song was such emotional bullshit that I couldn't stand it, couldn't stand myself.

But I shouldn't have taken that out on Rose tonight. That was some shitty behavior.

God, why was Rose so fucking *patient?* I was a complete asshole tonight and she was so goddamned sweet. I didn't deserve her. I pulled out my phone and typed out a text.

ME: Sorry for being a twat. I'm feeling shitty
but you didn't deserve my shittiness. Talk to
you tomorrow?

After a few moments, Rose replied with a simple heart emoji. Then:

ROSE: I get it. Talk to you tomorrow.

CHAPTER 11
More Than You'd Expect

Knock knock knock!

I looked up from where I was scrolling on my phone in bed. "Come in!" I called.

My bedroom door slammed open and Ducky stood in the hall. "Today's the day," she said. I caught a glimpse of Jem and Marlowe standing behind her.

"The day for what?" I asked.

"Girls trip to the sex shop!" Ducky yelled, pumping her fists in the air. Jem and Marlowe repeated the phrase until it became a chant, all three of them dancing in my doorway.

I laughed. "Give me a few minutes to get ready," I said.

Half an hour later, we had all piled into Jem's Subaru and driven to a favorite store of Ducky's in Berkley. ("We're supporting queer, femme-owned small businesses, not big box stores," she had said when giving Jem directions.)

The shop was squeezed between a chiropractor's office

and a café, and had a giant pride flag in the window. When we walked in, a bell chimed.

"Welcome in!" a voice said. I looked over to see a statuesque redhead stocking shelves. "Let me know if you need help finding anything!"

I glanced around. I'd never been in an actual sex shop before. Which was maybe a little strange, but I guess it made sense—I'd never had any need to before. And it was…overwhelming?

I followed the other girls past a display of handcuffs and whips. We walked past a tall shelving display full of realistic-looking dildos. (At least I assumed they were realistic. The only real penises I'd ever seen were in pornography or movies, and I had a feeling that that wasn't a realistic sampling.)

"Holy shit, this thing comes up to my waist!" Marlowe exclaimed. I looked over to see her standing next to a dildo that was at least three feet tall.

"Please tell me this is just for decoration," Jem said, her eyes widening.

"It's so realistic," Ducky said, almost reverently. She laid a hand gently on the top of it.

"That one's just for decoration," a voice said. I turned to see the tall redheaded woman from earlier. "But we do stock some that size for personal use. They're more novelty items than anything else but I'm not here to yuck any yums."

Ducky was still staring at the dildo statue. "I don't think any normal human could survive this."

"Can I help y'all find anything today?" the redhead asked. Her name tag said "Betty."

Marlowe slung an arm around my shoulder. "We need condoms and lube for—"

Jem cut her off by slapping a hand over her mouth. "We need condoms and lube," she said.

I gave Jem a silent smile of thanks. I didn't really need everyone in this shop knowing why I was here. Let them all think I did this all the time. I didn't want the extra attention.

"We've got all of that along the back wall," Betty said. "We just got a new line of water and silicone hybrid lube that I've been losing my mind about. And it's condom safe. Come this way."

So we all followed Betty as she led us to a wall of condoms. And honestly, I was grateful she was there. Because there were way too many options, and as much as I loved my friends, they were being a lot. We got some of the lube Betty recommended, plus three different kinds of condoms, just to have options.

We were making our way back to the front to pay when Ducky stopped me.

"Ooooh, we should get you a vibrator!" she exclaimed.

I felt my cheeks grow warm. "That's okay," I said.

Marlowe grabbed my arm. "Rose, I'm telling you. Vibrators are amazing."

"I really just need the…this stuff," I replied.

"Come on!" Marlowe wheedled. "I'll talk you through the different options. You can get a suction one or a wand or a bullet or a rabbit or—"

"I already have one," I mumbled at the floor.

Marlowe let go of my arm and grinned at me. "I thought you'd never been to a sex shop before!"

"I got it online," I whispered.

"Rose," Ducky said. "We are surrounded by fake penises right now. You don't have to whisper. There's literally nothing to be ashamed about."

"I'm not ashamed," I said. "I'm just…it's a little embarrassing."

"Okay, fine," Ducky said. "No vibrator. Do you want lingerie?"

I thought for a moment. "Maybe, but I don't want to buy it today," I said. I didn't want all of my girlfriends in *all* of my business, at least not at this point. It was starting to feel like my first time having sex was becoming a group project, and I wasn't really into that idea.

We made our way to the front and I handed over my purchases and debit card. I leaned against the counter and looked around again. On the ground next to me was some kind of, I don't know, seat? It looked like a cylinder cut in half, like you could put a saddle on it. There was a button on the counter nearby. And for some inexplicable reason, without a thought in my head, I pressed it.

The half-cylinder seat next to me roared to life, vibrating so intensely that it shook the countertop.

"Oh my god!" I yelled. I leapt back from the counter, the seat still rumbling. The condoms and lube on the countertop were jumping around from the vibration. Even the shelves nearby were shaking. Ducky finally lurched forward and pressed the button again, and the seat went still.

From the other end of the store, someone yelled, "Yeeeeee haw!"

I buried my face in my hands.

"So that's called a Sybian," Betty said. I could hear the smile in her voice.

"Thanks, Betty," Jem said. She grabbed the bag, grabbed my hand, and yanked us out of the store.

When we got out onto the sidewalk, all four of us looked at each other for a few long seconds. Then we all burst into laughter.

"Why would they put that button there?!" Marlowe laughed.

Ducky grabbed my arm. "Why the hell did you press it?"

"I don't know!" I exclaimed through giggles. "I don't know what happened! I saw a button and I just followed my instincts!"

Jem was laughing so hard she had her hands on her knees. She looked up at us. "What the fuck is a Sybian?" she asked.

"You can google it when we get home," Ducky said.

BACK AT OUR APARTMENT, I carried my purchases into my bedroom. I dumped the lube and condoms onto my bed and stared at them.

I supposed there was still a chance that it could be someone else that I used these things with. I could meet someone at a show somewhere and sparks could fly and we could end up back here.

But I couldn't picture it. I couldn't imagine anyone but Felix in my bed.

My phone buzzed, and when I turned it over, I saw a text from Felix on the screen.

FELIX: Do you have time to talk rn?

I dialed his number and laid back onto the pillows.

"Hey," he said.

"Hi."

Felix let out a long sigh. "I'm sorry I was such an asshole yesterday."

I started to say, "It's okay," but then remembered Jem's phrase about "acting in alignment with self-worth.

Instead, I said, "Thanks." When Felix didn't say anything more, I added, "Do you want to talk about it?"

Another long sigh. "I was in a bad mood when I got there. And when you asked me about songwriting stuff…I guess I'm still sensitive," Felix said. "About the whole Eva thing. And songwriting, I guess."

I closed my eyes. Of course he wasn't over Eva. Why would he be? She was perfect for him, with her alt-girl nose-ring and large-framed glasses and effortless style. Even all these years later, even when she was more of a ghost than a presence, I still couldn't live up to her.

"I'm sorry I brought it up," I said.

"Oh, *you're* fine," Felix said. "I'm the one who needs to grow the fuck up."

I smiled. "Have you ever written a song about that?" I asked.

"Growing the fuck up?" I heard Felix shifting, and I imagined him laying back on his bed. "Not yet. But I should."

"I think it'd be a great song," I replied.

"Have you ever tried songwriting again?" Felix asked. "Since college."

I shook my head, then remembered he couldn't see me and said, "No. But that's okay. I don't really want to write songs."

"I guess you write poetry instead, which is close," Felix said.

"I think that's how it's supposed to be," I said.

"What?"

"That all of us create differently. I can't play piano or write songs, but I write poetry. You're the opposite. And other people paint, and some people dance. Like all of us have this big impulse to just create, but everyone gets a different way to do it."

"Do you think stock brokers have the impulse to create?" Felix asked.

I rolled onto my stomach. "I don't know any stock brokers. Maybe they do, but they ignore it."

"And that's why we live in a capitalist hellscape. Because stock brokers should be painting and shit."

"Exactly," I smiled.

"Hey, Rose?"

"Yeah?" I said. Something in me did a little somersault at his saying my name.

"Thanks for putting up with my bullshit."

I laughed gently. "Thanks for putting up with mine."

"You literally don't have any."

"Jem says I need to work on setting boundaries," I replied.

"Everyone struggles with that."

I let myself sigh a small happy sigh, and settled into bed to talk more.

CHAPTER 12

The Best Friend a Guy Could Ask For

JUNIOR YEAR OF HIGH SCHOOL, AGE 16

FELIX

"I'm telling you," Xalia said. "The mic pack is going to fall out if I put it in my bra."

"There's literally no other place to put it," I said, handing the pack over.

"What about in my wig?" Xalia said.

Rose looked up from where she was ripping off strips of mic tape to hand to cast members. "If you put the mic pack in your wig and something goes wrong during the show, we can't get to it fast enough," she said.

"Besides," I added, "You're off stage for literally 30 seconds total over this whole show. It's easier to get to your bra than under your wig."

"Ugh, fine," Xalia replied, taking the pack from me. "But if it falls out during choreography, it's your fault."

"I'll take all the blame," I said.

Sammie, the student stage manager, poked their head

through the greenroom door. "Five minutes until top of show!"

A chorus of "Thank you five!" rose in response.

I pointed at Xalia. "Don't put your mic in your wig."

Xalia waited to see if Mrs. Tadema was around, then flipped me off.

"Break a leg," Rose said, then dragged me up to the sound booth. If anyone else had grabbed my sleeve and pulled me somewhere, I would have wanted to punch them in the face. But I didn't mind when Rose did it.

I sat down in front of the sound board. It was a miracle we got Xalia a working mic at all. The one she was assigned was a bust during mic check, so we'd had to dig up a spare one while she was getting into costume. We'd have to set levels and EQ during the opening number.

Mrs. Tadema looked up from her spot in the booth. "Did you get Xalia's mic to her?"

"She wanted to put it in her wig," I replied.

"We told her not to," Rose added. She pulled on a headset. This was the second school musical we'd run sound together for, and I didn't know how anyone did this job alone. Rose was in charge of playing cues, and I was in charge of mics. During the last show, we'd gotten it down to a perfect silent ballet.

Mrs. Tadema tried to have students do as much as possible—run sound, run lights, stage manage. She usually hung out in the booth in case of emergencies, but we hadn't had one as long as I'd been a student.

The first twenty minutes of the show went great. I was able to guess at levels before Xalia came onstage, so EQ-ing wasn't too hard.

But forty minutes into the show, Xalia was in the middle of singing when suddenly her voice cut out. Just for a moment—a couple of words. Then I could hear her again. I glanced behind me at the wall of receivers. Every-thing good there.

Then another few words gone. When Xalia spoke again, a sizzly crackle came through the speakers. A tell-tale sign of either a loose connection or moisture getting into the mic. Then I realized.

"Fuck, we didn't put a condom on it."

"Language," Mrs. Tadema's voice said over the headset.

"Sorry, latex sleeve," I said.

"Not what I meant."

Now there was more crackling than words.

"Shit shit shit," I murmured. I tried to turn her mic down so that the crackling wasn't as obvious, but then Xalia wasn't even audible over the tracks. We always put "latex sleeves" over the mic packs to protect them from sweat, but we'd been so busy arguing about the mic pack placement that we'd forgotten.

"Okay," Mrs. Tadema said. "Xalia's coming offstage for a quick change at the end of this song. Rose, go check the connection on the mic pack. Felix, run to the tech cabinet in the classroom and grab a latex sleeve for her."

"What about sound cues?" Rose asked.

"I've got it, just go."

Rose and I both threw our headsets off in unison. I flew down the stairs and down the hallway while Rose made her way backstage. In less than a minute, we were standing side by side in the wings, waiting for Xalia to come offstage.

When she did, Rose whispered desperately, "We need to check your mic pack."

Two other technicians were rushing through Xalia's costume change. She stared at both of us in horror. "It's in my wig," she replied.

"Oh my god," I said. I glanced out onto the stage. We had roughly fifteen seconds before Xalia had to be out there again. One of the technicians was finishing tying one of Xalia's shoes.

Then Rose stepped behind Xalia and yanked out two wig pins. She stuck them in her mouth, lifted the wig from behind, and pulled the mic pack out. She checked the connection between the lavalier cord and the mic pack, then plugged it more firmly in. She held her hand out for the condom and pulled it on, then handed Xalia the pack and shoved the wig pins back into her hair.

All of it took less than eight seconds.

"What am I supposed to—?" Xalia asked, holding her mic pack.

Rose pulled down Xalia's shirt and stuffed the mic pack down it, clipping it to her bra.

Xalia was still walking out onstage when she said her first line.

But she made it.

Holy shit. I looked at Rose, then in mock dramatic fashion, I collapsed onto the ground in relief. A quiet hysterical laugh escaped me.

"Are you okay?" Rose asked. Her smiling face appeared above me, blocking my view of the catwalks above the stage.

"That was amazing," I replied. "You are so fast at putting condoms on."

Even in the dim light, I saw Rose's face redden. I hadn't meant to say it like that, so I quickly course corrected.

"That whole thing was so fast, Rose," I added. "If ever we're in some kind of war, I'm sticking by you."

"Come on," Rose said, holding her hand out. I took it and let her haul me up. After we were both upright, we stood across from each other for a moment. Rose's soft, warm brown eyes tilted up at me. Her long hair was up in a bun, but she'd pulled some of it out and it was framing her face in a way I'd never noticed before. Actually, did she have bangs? How long had she had bangs? I was about to ask when I had another realization. I frowned down at her.

"Have you always been this short?" I whispered.

Rose shook her head. "You got taller over the summer," she replied.

"Huh," I replied. It occurred to me that Rose and I almost never stood this close to each other. If we did, it was usually side by side. How had I not noticed that I was a full head taller than her now? If I were to wrap my arms around her, I could tuck her head right under my chin. She would fit perfectly.

"Aren't you supposed to be in the booth?" a voice whispered. I turned to see one of the deck hands looking at us.

"Shit, we gotta get back up there," I said. I stepped away from Rose, and without thinking, I grabbed her hand. "Let's go." I pulled her along down the hallway, back up the stairs, and into the tech booth. I didn't realize we'd been holding hands the whole time until I had to let go to put my headset back on.

Mrs. Tadema scooted out of the way, letting me sit in front of the sound board again. I turned my attention to the stage, where Xalia was singing, her mic working perfectly now.

"Was it the connection?" Mrs. Tadema asked over the headset.

"Yep," Rose replied. "It was loose. And Felix was able to get the latex sleeve."

Somehow Rose managed to say all of this while still hitting cues on the computer. I unmuted the mics for the number that was starting and looked up to find Rose smiling at me.

How did I live without her before this? By comparison, Freshman year was a blurry nightmare until Rose came along. Rose, with her music and her calm and her compassion.

The best friend a guy could ask for.

CHAPTER 13

Sunday Fun Day

ROSE

"Jesus *fuck* that's so many sprinkles!" Felix exclaimed.

Wendy didn't look up from the casserole dish on the table, where roughly two gallons of ice cream were currently piled. "Stop complaining," he admonished.

"No, this is out of control," Felix said. "The proportions are gonna be way off. We need more chocolate syrup."

He glanced around the table and grabbed the bottle. Simon grabbed his hair dramatically. "It's gonna overflow!" he warned.

"We'll catch it!" Ducky exclaimed, hands at the ready.

I laughed. I had no doubt that Ducky really would try to catch an overflowing ice cream sundae with her bare hands. "We need a bigger dish," I commented.

Jem ran to the kitchen and came back with a handful of spoons. "Not if we eat it fast enough!"

Within minutes, the room took on the chaotic joy of a children's birthday party, as eight fully grown adults each grabbed a spoon to eat from our communal Sunday sundae.

Moments like this sometimes took me by grateful surprise. I'd spent so much of my life feeling so lonely. And then every now and then, I found myself in the middle of all this laughter-filled love. There was Jem, looking so badass with her colored hair and her tattoos, organizing everything around her. Ducky, in all of her glorious chaos. Marlowe, somehow sweet and badass all at once, a rebel with so much compassion. I was so lucky.

And then the boys, who had all made their way into my heart over the past year. Aaron, with his handsome brawny-ness and innocence. Simon, all rock star god and upright morals. Enigmatic Wendy and his insane drumming.

And Felix. The best boy I'd ever known. Black nail polish and eyeliner and the most creative and sensitive soul. Long sculpted body and dark black hair. Here next to me, eating ice cream with all these other people we loved.

He caught me looking at him. "What?" he asked.

I shrugged, giving him a small smile. "Just grateful," I said.

"You've got chocolate..." Felix said. I watched as his eyes dropped to my mouth. In a slow, smooth gesture, he reached out and swiped a thumb over my lower lip.

I stopped breathing.

Felix's green eyes stayed glued to mine as he lifted his thumb and sucked it into his mouth. And suddenly I could feel my heartbeat between my legs.

"Wanna come to my room?" I whispered. I'm pretty sure I sounded as desperate as I felt.

Felix's pupils dilated. He set down his spoon, and then took mine out of my hand. I don't know if anyone even noticed as he dragged me down the hallway. But I didn't care.

The second my bedroom door was shut, Felix pressed me against it, the whole heated length of him pinning me in place. His hand reached up to my jaw and then his mouth was on mine.

This wasn't anything like before. This was frantic and heated, some kind of hurried hunger driving both of us. Felix's tongue swept into my mouth, and I was vaguely aware of a strangled moan escaping me.

The sound of it seemed to do something to Felix. He lifted me off my feet, and by instinct, my legs came up around his waist. I didn't think I could stop kissing him if I tried. I didn't want to.

And then we were on my bed, and his weight was hovering over me. Felix's head dipped down as he pressed his lips along my jaw, down the column of my throat, along the tops of my breasts. My back arched into his kisses. Somehow, from the tangle of our bodies, I reached down to grab the bottom of my tank top. And then Felix's hands were there, helping me pull it off over my head, leaving me in just my shorts and bra. I thought briefly of the lingerie I had just gotten, sitting in one of my dresser drawers, and for a moment I mourned the fact that I was wearing just a regular old t-shirt bra. But then I looked into Felix's face and forgot to mourn anything.

His arms were bracketed on either side of my head. I wanted more of him. I wanted skin. I reached for the hem of his t-shirt, looking into his face. He nodded, then helped me pull it off.

And then his bare chest and stomach were there in front of me. I ran a fingertip over his collarbones, then spread my palm wide over one of his pecs. I reached up to cover the other one, then moved my hands down over his stomach.

I'd seen Felix without a shirt before. Every time, I'd had to be intentional about my gaze, trying not to linger. He wasn't especially muscular, just surprisingly toned. Thin, but strong.

And now, by some miracle, I got to run my hands over his torso. When I brought my gaze back to Felix's face, his eyes were closed, his mouth open. I watched his breath hitch as I moved my hands back up, brushing over his nipples in the process. Was I…was I actually turning him on?

I pulled him down on top of me, finding his mouth again. My legs fell open to him. I felt drunk with power, drunk with pleasure. After a few more moments, my hips tilted up, my body throbbing with need.

Felix slotted one of his legs between mine. As soon as his thigh was pressed up against the core of me, I ground against it, seeking connection, seeking friction, seeking *something*. My whole body was vibrating with want. Locked in frantic kisses, I fumbled to find Felix's hand and then brought it to my breast.

Felix's hand squeezed, and he moaned into my mouth, low and quiet. And suddenly all I wanted was all of him, right now, right here. I reached down to his belt and with shaking fingers, unbuckled it. Felix's mouth left mine and he mumbled something, but I was too preoccupied to hear what. I undid the top button of his pants. My fingers found his zipper and started to pull it down. I couldn't quite tell, but I thought I brushed against the hardness of him, heated and aching.

"Wait. Wait, Rose, hold on," Felix muttered. Then he grabbed my wrist. "Rose. Wait."

I froze. Felix was looking down at me, his breath

ragged. I finally fully comprehended that he was telling me to stop. Because of course he was. Because he wasn't actually into me. I was just a friend. And I was practically mauling him. Hot waves of embarrassment flooded me. "Oh my god," I said. My free hand flew to cover my face. "Oh my god, I'm sorry!"

"No, it's okay," Felix said. "Rose, stop. Really." I felt him shift so that he was laying beside me. His voice was devastatingly soft when he spoke again. "Rose, look at me."

I was mortified. I had just let my lust or whatever run away with me. I had acted like a woman possessed.

"Rose," Felix said again.

I took a deep breath. *It's Felix*, I reminded myself. I uncovered my face and turned my head so that I was facing him. I bit my lip.

"Sorry I kind of…lost my mind a little bit," I whispered.

Felix gave me one of his rare, tender smiles. "Honestly, it was kind of awesome. I'll take it as a compliment," he said. He reached out and brushed some of my hair off my forehead, and the act was so intimate that my eyes almost fluttered closed.

Instead, I studied Felix's face. "Then why did you stop me?" I asked.

Felix turned so that he was laying on his back next to me. I was feeling too embarrassed to let my eyes skate over his body. He stared up at the ceiling. "Because," he said. His words were slow and measured. "Because if we do this, I want you to be sure. I want it to be something you think about and make a decision about. Not just something that happens because it feels good in the moment."

I turned and looked at the ceiling, too. I couldn't bring myself to look at Felix as I whispered my next words. "I thought you weren't into it. With me."

"Rose," Felix said.

I found the courage to turn my head. His striking eyes found mine. "Any guy would be *insane* to not be into it with you."

My heart seemed to freeze in my chest for a moment before it began beating wildly. I didn't know what to say.

Felix raised himself up on one elbow to look at me. My eyes drifted down over his body, lingering on the thin trail of dark hair that disappeared into his briefs. His belt was still unbuckled, the top button of his pants undone, the zipper half pulled down. Even when not in the heat of the moment, I still longed to unzip his pants further, shove them down over his hips, see more of him.

I forced my gaze back up to his face. "I think…" I started, swallowing. "I'm pretty sure I've already made my decision. I'm pretty sure I want to."

Felix looked at me, and then collapsed back down at my side. Then he turned his face to me.

"How about this?" he said. "Give it twenty-four hours. Long enough to cool down a little, really think about it. Make a pros and cons list." I giggled. "If you still want to by…" He glanced at his watch. "Seven forty-two tomorrow, text me."

That time would be etched into my whole body forever. "Deal," I nodded. I heard laughter coming from the kitchen. "Should we…go back out there?"

Felix smiled at me and sat up. "Come on," he said. I grabbed my shirt and pulled it back on, and tried to act like I wasn't looking at him doing the same. I watched his fingers as they buttoned his pants and buckled his belt.

When our hair was fixed and our breathing was normal, we went to rejoin our friends.

CHAPTER 14

Twenty-four Hours

FELIX

I told Rose to think about it for twenty-four hours, so that she was sure.

But if I was being completely honest with myself, I think *I* needed those twenty-four hours, too.

After the guys and I all left Sundae Sunday, I shut my bedroom door and sat down at the piano. Both because I didn't really want to hear from them about Rose and I disappearing into her bedroom for a while, and because music always helped me sort my shit out.

And I had some shit to sort out. I wanted to be sure. About the offer I made to Rose. I wanted to weigh our friendship into the equation, figure out the risks.

I moved my fingers over the keys, a slow meandering melody coming together. After a few minutes, I started putting words to it.

I move my fingers over the keys

> *The way your hands moved on my skin*
> *Like there's music just beneath the surface*
> *That makes me want to let you in*
>
> *Your rosy lips, your tender hands*
> *The way your breathing lifts your breasts*

Shit. This wasn't helping me focus. I held my head in my hands for a moment, then stood up and left the apartment, making my way to Alameda Beach.

Now, with the soft sand under my feet and Billy Joel playing in my earbuds, I stuck my hands in my pockets and let my mind work through the last couple of hours.

Things had gotten so hot so fast. All I did was wipe a little chocolate off of her lip (her perfect lip) and then I was like, possessed. Her skin felt so good. *All* of her felt so good. I hadn't thought about "education" when I shoved her against her bedroom door. There was no part of me that thought, *Oh, Rose might want to know what it feels like to be pinned against a door.* I did it because I wanted to. Because she looked so pretty and so kissable and I wanted my hands and lips on her.

And then she made that stifled moaning sound and all I could think about was getting her onto the bed. I thought about the way she moved her hands over my chest and stomach when my shirt was gone. Dear god, I didn't think anyone had ever touched me like that? Like I was being worshipped. I was hard by the time she did that, and when she started grinding on my thigh, I thought I was going to lose my mind. With my hand on her breast and my tongue in her mouth, I truly didn't know how I managed to stop her from taking my pants off.

Because at that moment, I had really really *really* wanted her to take my pants off. I had wanted to shove the cups of her bra down and yank her shorts off and bury myself in every part of her. There was nothing measured or thoughtful about it.

What the fuck had happened?

Part of me felt a little bit guilty for stopping her the way I did—I didn't want her to feel embarrassed or like she'd violated consent or something. But somewhere in the back of my mind, I had thought, *If Rose and I fumble into this right now, we're both going to regret it.* And I knew it was true. I knew *I'd* regret it, at least. I didn't want her first time to be some hasty, hormone-driven thing. And if I was going to be the first person she did it with, I wanted to be in my right mind, too. And I knew Rose. I knew she did things patiently and deliberately, and that sex shouldn't be any different

Rose. Goddamn.

Who knew she could kiss like that? In a way that scrambled my thoughts and filled me with want? I'd made out with some good kissers before, and had sex with people who were good at sex. But this was the first time I could remember it feeling like…that.

I glanced out over the bay, the San Francisco skyline glittering in the distance. I was glad Rose's official first kiss was here, on Alameda Beach. That felt like a gift I could give her. Some small thing I could do to repay her for all of the hundreds (thousands?) of times she'd been there for me.

And maybe I could do the same when it came to sex. I could make her first time a good experience—something safe and communicative. I could make sure it was with someone she knew and trusted, someone who would listen to her and check in with her, who wouldn't make her do anything she didn't want to do.

When I thought about it that way, it felt genuinely selfless. Sure, I was also getting something enjoyable out of the deal, but this wasn't about me. It was about Rose. I just had to make sure that she held the steering wheel, the whole time.

Because if I tried to hold it, I thought, *we might crash.*

I shook my head to dismiss the thought, then glanced at my watch. 9:43. Roughly twenty-two hours until Rose made her decision.

I paused. I hoped she didn't feel pressured. I didn't want her to think she *had* to do this, just because it was the chance that was in front of her. Now that I thought about it, maybe I was actually depriving her of a great experience, by not allowing her to have it with someone she was actually dating. Maybe I was being a selfish prick after all. As usual.

I pulled out my phone and sent Rose a text.

> ME: Hey, please know you don't have to have sex with me if you don't want to. If you want to wait until you're actually dating someone to have that first experience, I swear I won't be offended. I'm down if you're down, but don't feel pressured.

I hit send, then read over it and sighed. I was such a fuckup when it came to expressing myself, but I trusted that Rose could figure out what I was trying to say.

Her reply came through a few seconds later.

> ROSE: Thanks. Thanks for giving me time to think about it. I trust we'll still be friends no matter what.

I felt relief move through my chest. I didn't know why I was freaking out so much. Rose was Rose. When I was around her, everything felt like it was in the right place.

She's been the one keeping my hands on the wheel this whole time anyway.

Another message came in.

ROSE: Talk to you at 7:42 tomorrow.

I smiled, put my phone back in my pocket, and kept walking.

CHAPTER 15

7:42 PM

ROSE

Right after Felix left last night, I walked to my room, shut the door, and started pacing. I felt frantic, certain that he would change his mind. I already knew I wanted all of him. I kept resisting the urge to text him right then that I didn't need to wait twenty-four hours, I already knew.

But by the next afternoon, I was far enough away from the memory of his body against mine that I felt a little calmer. Calm enough to at least approach this twenty-four hour thing in good faith. I glanced at my phone. 3:27 pm. I remembered Felix's joking recommendation to make a pros and cons list, so I sat down at my desk with my notebook.

Pros of Having Sex With Felix
1. Having sex with Felix
2. Don't have to feel dumb for not having done it at my age

3. First time can be with someone I trust

<u>*Cons of Having Sex With Felix*</u>
*1. He's more experienced and that might actu-
ally be a bad thing? Like, I might feel embarrassed that I don't know stuff*
2. I might get my heart broken really badly

I sat back. Really, everything I was thinking and feeling fell under the umbrella of the things I had listed. But when it came down to it, it was really just a battle between the pro of "having sex with Felix" and the con of "I might get my heart broken really badly."

My heart was already lined with cracks from all the times it had broken for Felix. But when I thought about the tender way he had kissed my neck, the way his hand felt on my breast, his lips against mine, then the answer was so obvious that I didn't know how I could choose any other option.

The closer it got to 7:42 pm, the more nervous I felt. I agonized over how to phrase the text. But the second the clock switched over to that exact time, I hit send.

> ME: I made my decision and I'd like to go for it if you're still down

I could hardly breathe while I waited for his response. It came in seconds.

> FELIX: Should I come over right now?

Oh my god. *Oh my god.* I was grinning so hard I thought my face might break. I truly wanted him to come over right this second, but I also hadn't showered yet today, and that seemed important. I typed out a reply.

ME: Meet at my place at 8:42

At 8:41, a knock came on the door. I opened it to find Felix standing on the doorstep. Black tight pants. Black t-shirt. Black button-up. My heart was hammering in my chest. I thought about the matching bra and panty lingerie set I was wearing beneath my clothes and wanted Felix in my room more than ever.

"You never knock," I said.

"I'm a minute early," he replied.

"That's okay," I said. "I'm ready."

He followed me inside. "Marlowe's at my place with Simon," he said. "Where are Ducky and Jem?"

"At a show in Berkley," I replied. We were both walking so fast that by the time I'd finished speaking, we'd reached my bedroom. We stepped inside and I closed the door behind us.

Felix and I stood and looked at each other. His eyes were tender, but I thought I saw a hint of apprehension in them. "Are you sure?" he asked.

I replied by stepping into him and pulling his mouth down toward mine.

I walked him backwards and then pushed him down onto my bed. I thought I saw a faint red flush rise in Felix's cheeks, and the sight made me bold. I climbed over him until my knees were on either side of his ribs, Felix's body hot and strong beneath me. I leaned down to kiss him again. The fabric of my short skirt was gathered on his stomach, and I was deeply aware of his fly pressing up into my panties. His hands tangled into my hair, then ran down my neck, over my chest, around my hips. I was drowning in him and it was so perfect, I thought I might die. I sat up enough to pull my shirt over my head, but before I could lean down to kiss Felix again, he stopped me.

"What?" I asked, feeling suddenly anxious.

Felix's eyes were fixed on my breasts. I watched him take in the red lace of my bra, the way it pushed up what little I had to a satisfying roundness.

"Fucking damn," Felix whispered. Then he reached up both hands to cup me, massaging me gently. "This is a great fucking bra," he murmured, his hands working me. My eyes fluttered closed, and I couldn't stop my hips from rolling. The friction on my most sensitive spot was torturous. I let my hips roll again.

"Wait," Felix said, moving his hands down to my waist. I almost cried. "Before we keep going, I just want to check in. When you say you want to have sex, does that mean that you want me inside of you?"

My breath caught.

"Yes," I whispered.

"What part of me?" Felix asked. His voice was low and it sent my blood humming.

I swallowed. "Your cock."

"Inside what part of you?"

Had Felix's voice always had that husky tone?

"My pussy," I said, too turned on to feel awkward about the word.

"Okay," he said. "I brought a few different brands of condoms. And lube."

"I have those, too," I said, looking down at him. "Will you please keep touching me?"

Felix's hands moved back up to my breasts, and after a moment or two, I reached behind my back and undid the clasp of my bra. Then I watched Felix's eyes as I slid the fabric off my skin, leaving my body bare.

He took me in. I watched him bite his lip, and then he reached out and brushed a thumb over my nipple.

I cried out and braced myself against his chest, my thighs clenching around him in pleasure. Felix reached up with his other hand to touch me the same way on the other side.

"If something doesn't feel good, you tell me," he said. His voice sounded hoarse.

I nodded. "I will." His thumbs kept gently moving over my nipples and my eyes closed at the sensation. "Can I tell you when something *does* feel good?" I asked, breathless.

"Please," Felix replied.

"This feels good," I whispered. I opened my eyes to find him grinning at me. I thought of us in my bed yesterday, the long lines of his bare chest and stomach.

"Can I take your shirt off, please?" I managed.

When he nodded, I scooted down enough to let him sit up. I shoved his button-up shirt down his shoulders and lifted his shirt off. I couldn't believe that I got to do this, that I *finally* got to do this. When he was laying back again, I ran my hand over his chest. Felix's palms slid up my thighs until they were clutching my hips, his hands up under my skirt. When I ground against him again, I felt the hardness of him between my legs. My blood was roaring.

"Shit, you feel good, Rose," he said.

It was like I was seeing stars. I leaned down to kiss him, my bare tits pressed against the bare skin of his chest. It felt so good I could barely think. We kissed like that for a long time, before Felix rolled us so that I was on my back. He grasped my wrists and pushed my arms up over my head, causing me to gasp. He kissed down my neck, and then his lips were on the hardened points of my tits, wet and hot and greedy.

I writhed beneath him, a hungry sound escaping me. I wanted to feel more of him.

"I want to touch you," I said.

"What part of me?" Felix murmured.

"Your cock."

He smiled up at me and then released my hands. He placed his knees on the bed on either side of my legs, letting me undo the button of his pants. I slid the zipper down and reached inside, palming him over his briefs.

His dick was so hard that I could feel him straining against the fabric. I looked up into his face. "Can I take it out?" I asked.

Felix studied me for a long moment, then nodded. I pushed his briefs down over his hips, and then he was free, the whole hard length of him, a dark tuft of hair at the base. I didn't know if it was because I was more turned on than I ever had been in my life, or because it was Felix, but I loved the sight of it. I wrapped my hand around him experimentally.

Felix made an involuntary sound and then thrust slowly into my fist. "Fffuck," he hissed.

A blinding hot need pulsed between my legs. I swallowed hard. "Do you want to get a condom?" I whispered. "And lube?"

"Is it too soon?" Felix replied. "We don't have to do it right away."

I shook my head. "I'm ready now. I feel…I just…I want it now."

Felix got out of bed, and shoved his pants and briefs down the rest of the way, while I wriggled out of my skirt and underwear. I caught a glimpse of Felix's ass as he bent down to pull a condom out of his pants pocket. I grinned. It was a good ass. I'd always thought so in all the years I'd seen it being hugged by his tight pants. It looked good out of his pants, too.

While he rolled the condom on, I reached into my nightstand drawer and pulled out the lube. When I turned back to Felix, it was to find him staring at me. He had a look in his eyes I'd never seen before. It was vulnerable and hungry and surprised. I was already naked, but this made me feel even more so.

"What is it?" I asked.

Felix smiled and gave his head a small shake. "You're beautiful," he said. He said it simply, matter-of-factly. And it felt like fireworks in my bones. He had never said that to me. I spent so many years thinking he never would.

"Th-thanks," I managed.

Felix knelt on the bed and took the lube from me. I watched him coat the palm of his hand and then stroke himself, once, twice. A third time. And the sight of it was making me feel insane with lust, like my insides were vibrating. If I wasn't so desperate to have him, I would want to watch him do that more. But there was so much desire coursing through my body that I didn't want to delay the next part for a second longer.

Felix poured more lube onto his fingers and then looked at me before reaching down between my legs.

The feeling of his fingers against me caused a moan to escape my lips. Felix's touch slid over my most sensitive spot, then gently moved to my entrance. My sense of need intensified as he rose to kneeling again.

I let my legs fall open and Felix settled himself between them. He looked up at my face, one of his hands still stroking his cock slowly. My heart hammered a rhythm with my thoughts.

This is happening, this is happening, this is happening.

"It shouldn't hurt," Felix whispered, breathless. "If it does, tell me and I'll pull out."

I nodded and rested my hands on his shoulders. Felix bent down to kiss my lips, his tongue driving my need even higher.

Still, he didn't enter me. He let his mouth roam over my neck, down my chest, his tongue lingering on my nipples again. His kisses were torturous. I was practically blind with want.

"Please, Felix," I whimpered.

I felt him press against my entrance, and then slowly, so slowly, Felix pushed himself inside. I almost sobbed at how good it felt. After one brief, shaking moment, he stayed there, letting me adjust.

"Good?" he asked, his voice low.

I nodded. It was perfect—it was so much pleasure that any more of it would have been pain. I had the sensation of being filled with exactly what I needed. Felix drew his hips back and then pushed slowly forward again. My eyes closed with the perfection of it, and a sighing moan escaped me. On his next thrust, my hips tilted to meet him.

CHAPTER 16

Sex Quest Questions

FELIX

The way I was responding, you'd think it was *my* first time. When I sank into Rose, my whole body shuddered with pleasure. Sex usually felt great, but this was something different. Maybe it was because we'd known each other so long? There was already so much trust there that the connection felt more intense.

I thrust into her again, and Rose let out this breathy moan that turned me on so much that I could barely stop myself from driving my hips harder into her. Even as I kept a steady pace, I could feel heat gathering, hear my breath getting ragged. Rose ran her hands over my shoulders, down my back, over my arms. I looked down at her, her eyes closed in pleasure, her lips parted and swollen.

Gorgeous, I thought. The word came into my mind unbidden.

A faint pink flush was spread over Rose's body, spreading up her neck in a way that made me even hungrier for her. I buried my face in her shoulder, sucking gently at her skin. She turned her head to give me better access.

God, she smelled so good. She *tasted* so good. I wanted to know what the rest of her tasted like…the soft skin of her thighs, the spot between her legs…

Slow down, Felix, I thought. *Let her be in charge.* Actually, I could do that right now, too. And maybe it would be easier for me to keep the pace if she was in charge.

Through some massive amount of willpower, I pulled out. Rose looked up at me with pleading eyes. "Why did you stop?" she asked.

"Because I have two questions," I gasped. Jesus, I sounded like I had been running a marathon.

"What?"

"Do you want to come? Like, is it important to you to orgasm during this?"

Rose looked up at me, her chest heaving. "If you keep doing what you were doing, I might come whether I try to or not."

Holy fuck Jesus shit. Why was Rose so hot all of a sudden.

"Okay," I said. "Do you want to try being on top?"

Rose flashed me a sudden smile, bright and heated. She nodded.

I rolled onto my back and watched as Rose slung one leg over me. (Damn, her *body*. Had it just been there like that, under her clothes, the whole time?) After another rub down with lube, I grasped my cock and then slowly guided Rose down onto it. I watched as her head tipped back, as her fingers curled against the bare skin of my chest.

"Just follow your instincts," I whispered. Rose rolled her hips experimentally and let out another one of those breathy moans. When she started riding me in earnest, I reached out to clutch her hips.

I don't know why the hell I thought I'd be able to have better control like this. Her perfect small tits were bouncing slightly as she rode me, her thighs surprisingly strong on either side of my ribs. She looked so good on top. Suddenly, I was *determined* to make her come.

I reached one hand down and brushed my thumb over her clit. When she cried out, I drew my hand back, but she reached out to grab my wrist. "Do that again," she whispered.

So I did, matching her speed as she went faster and faster, and then suddenly she was clenching her legs around me, her eyes squeezed shut, her mouth thrown open in ecstasy. The sight of it sent me over the edge, and I gasped out my release as she finished riding her own wave.

A few more pulsing moments from each of us, and then Rose collapsed onto my chest. We stayed like that until our breathing had slowed down, and then she gently slid off of me. I truly wanted nothing more than to stay right there, but there was the condom to take care of. I sat up and pulled it off, grabbing some tissues from Rose's bedside table to finish cleaning myself up. When I turned to look at her again, she was laying with her eyes closed, a languid smile on her lips. She looked so *satisfied*. With the house plants and succulents surrounding her bed, she looked like some kind of mystical forest goddess.

I'm not much of a cuddler. I don't really do pillow talk, and I'm not one to take the time to "emotionally connect" or whatever after sex. But I climbed into bed next to Rose and gathered her into my arms. She nestled her head against my chest. She fit so perfectly there.

"So, how was your first time?" I asked softly.

Rose was quiet for so long that for a second, I was worried it had been horrible and I just hadn't noticed somehow. But when she spoke, it was in a contented whisper. "It was perfect," she said. "It was exactly what I've always wanted."

"Good," I said. Thank god. And I wasn't going to lie, I was feeling pretty good about myself. I gave Rose the first time experience that she'd always wanted—trusting and enjoyable. Hell, she even *came*. I let my fingertips move gently up and down her spine.

"How was *your* first time?" Rose asked.

"Uhhhh…"

"Actually, *when* was your first time?"

Why did it feel weird to talk about this right now? Like we were inviting other women into the room or something. I spoke fast. "Freshman year of college, met her at a party, it was not like this, but it wasn't terrible." Somehow I could sense Rose smiling. "What?" I asked.

"I'm just really glad that *this* was not terrible." She sighed happily and wrapped an arm around me. Our bodies fit so well together. Even when we weren't actively having sex, it felt good to have her there against me. Like it was where she was *supposed* to be. I stared up at the ceiling, just listening to Rose breathing, feeling her soft bare skin.

"Can I ask you something?" Rose said.

"Yeah?"

"I guess I want to know…" she started. Then she was quiet.

"No dumb questions," I said.

"I um…I liked watching you…touch yourself," she said, haltingly. "When you were putting lube on?"

That…was not what I had expected her to say. I had a sudden vision of Rose sitting on the bed, watching me, biting her lip as I stroked my cock faster and faster. In my mind, her hand reached down between her own legs as she watched…

My heart thudded in my chest. "Yeah?" I said. "Is that…what's your question?"

"I guess I want to know if that's weird," she said.

"That I touched myself or that you liked it?"

"That I liked it."

"Not weird," I said. Possibly a little too quickly. "And even if it is weird, I don't care. Or like, no one should care. There's no such thing as normal."

"Okay, good," Rose said. She nuzzled into me again. "It's kind of nice to have someone I can ask sex questions."

"You can't ask Queen Anne?"

Rose shrugged in my arms. "I guess I could. They took me to a sex shop when I told them we might do this."

I raised my eyebrows. "How was that?"

Rose lifted her head to look at me. "Oh my god, Felix, I accidentally turned on this machine that was so loud!"

"You turned on a machine?"

"It was this vibrator…seat…thing. It like, rattled the windows."

"How did you turn it on *accidentally*?"

"I really have no explanation," Rose said, settling her head back down. "I saw a button and I pressed it."

I chuckled. "That's kind of incredible," I said.

"It really was."

"Well, feel free to ask me any sex questions," I said. "Sex questions for your sex quest."

"Sex quest questions!" Rose replied, a smile in her voice.

I laughed again. Then my eyes wandered to the scraps of red lace that were on the floor. "Is that where you got that red number?" I asked. "From the sex shop?"

"No," Rose said. "I got that online. At that point, we had already talked about lubes and condoms and vibrators and I was kind of done being vulnerable."

"The vibrator seat or other vibrators?"

"Technically both."

"Wait, do you have a vibrator?" I asked.

Rose paused, then I felt her nod her head.

Okay. I knew Rose had a threshold for vulnerability. But now I really wanted to know more about the vibrator thing. My mind was flooded with questions. What kind of vibrator did Rose have? What color? What shape? How often did she use it? What did she look like when she used it? Was it—

Calm down, you pervert, I admonished myself. Maybe sometime in the future we could talk about vibrators, but right now was not the time for Twenty Questions about Rose's Vibrator. Right now was about Rose and her experience.

"Hey," I said softly.

"Hmmm?" Rose said. Her voice sounded sleepy.

"How do you feel?" I asked. "Are you sore at all?"

"If I am, it's a good kind of sore," Rose replied. After a pause, she added, "Do you have to be anywhere tonight?"

I shook my head. "We can just hang out for a while," I said.

"Good," Rose replied. She tilted up to place a soft kiss on the side of my neck, and I felt myself melt a little. "Let's just stay like this for a little while."

I pulled her closer to me and let my eyes fall closed, a faint smile playing over my lips.

CHAPTER 17

The Wreck of the Sujameco

ROSE

Marlowe laugh-screamed as the cold waves washed over her feet. "Holy fuck, that's freezing!" she exclaimed.

"Don't talk shit about the Pacific Ocean!" Ducky replied. But she screamed just as loudly when the next wave hit.

I stood with Felix a few feet away while the others ran into the water and out again. I couldn't imagine Felix yanking off his black boots to jump around in the ocean, and I didn't really feel like joining in either. I was content to just watch this newly combined group of friends.

"Wanna go for a walk?" Felix asked. He nodded his head up the beach.

"Sure," I replied.

As I walked away, I could hear Wendy asking if he

should eat something he had just found, and I shook my head and laughed quietly.

"God, they're so chaotic," Felix said, looking over his shoulder. "Is that seaweed?"

I turned to see Simon holding something out of Wendy's reach. "I think it's kelp," I said. The voices of the others faded as we kept walking.

"I think I like the chaos," I said. "It kind of reminds me of high school drama class."

"We're too old for chaos," Felix grumbled.

I smiled to myself. Felix was famously the grumpiest person I knew. But I'd learned over the years that when Felix was extra grumpy, it was because he was feeling extra affection. He just didn't ever like showing it.

I looked up the beach, watching the grasses higher up the shore billowing and waving in the wind. Dotted along the sand, small groups of people were gathered with beach towels and umbrellas. I thought of the other members of Felix and I's bands, jumping around in the water behind us. Felix and I had known each other for so long, but for some reason we didn't really spend that much time at each other's houses. I'd met his fellow bandmates a few times, but this trip was the first time I was really getting to know them. Aaron, with his good looks and gullibility. Simon, the rock god. Wendy, who was still kind of a mystery to me, but I was learning that he was kind of a mystery to everyone. In the week and a half that we had been on tour together, they'd all made their way into my heart.

"It's kind of strange that I didn't really know the other guys before now," I said.

Felix shrugged. "It's weird that I didn't know the rest of Queen Anne before now."

"We should all hang out more," I said. "After the tour, I mean."

Felix didn't reply, but bent down to pick something up from the sand. He turned it over in his palm and then showed it to me. "Indian head penny," he said.

I took it from him, then turned it over to look at the date. "1905," I said. "How did you get here?" I asked the penny.

"There's a shipwreck from the twenties somewhere on this beach. It's probably from that."

I looked up at Felix. Only he could mention something like a century-old shipwreck so casually.

"There's a shipwreck? Here?"

"You can see it better at low tide," he replied. "And in the winter." He started walking again and I fell into step beside him. I started to hand him the penny, but he waved me away. "Keep it," he said.

I slipped the penny into my pocket, and my foolish heart knew that I probably *would* keep it. A souvenir, not just of the tour, but of this walk. I knew I was being senti-mental, but I couldn't help it.

"What's the story of the shipwreck?" I asked.

"It was a cargo ship," Felix said. "The Sujameco. It ran aground in the fog, and the crew survived, so they tried to get it out to sea again, but eventually they just had to abandon it. A lot of it got scrapped for metal in World War II, but the hull and some other parts are still there."

"How did you know that?"

"Because everyone bullied me in seventh grade so I sat in the library and read books about shipwrecks."

Felix didn't talk much about his life before we met. I knew he hadn't had a very happy childhood, and it made me ache with love for him even more when I thought about it. I didn't have a lot of friends growing up either, but that had more to do with my own shyness than anything else. I wasn't ever really bullied, just sort of left out. Which was its own kind of pain at times, but I usually had at least one friend. I wished I could have given Felix that same gift.

"If I had known you in seventh grade," I said. "I would have been your friend."

"You're my friend now," Felix said. He threw an arm around my shoulder and kissed my temple briefly. Then he dropped his arm and kept walking.

My heart squeezed in my chest. I was trying very hard to remain upright. He had never, in all the years I had known him, done anything like that. He'd hugged me before. But his quick and casual show of affection just now was so much more. The feeling of it was singing through me. It felt like bouquets of gold were blossoming inside of me, warming my chest, and I knew that as long as I lived, I wouldn't be able to find the right words for what that moment meant to me.

There was an exact moment in high school when I fell in love with Felix. In my memory, there was an audible click when it happened. It was junior year, and we were backstage at a musical. We'd just helped Xalia fix her mic (with seconds to spare), and Felix had fallen onto the ground with relief, which was adorable. When I had helped him up, he had just looked at me for a moment. And in that moment, with his green eyes looking down at me, I had truly and fully fallen in love with him. *Click.* It wasn't exactly a shocking revelation—I'd known my feelings for Felix were a little more than friendly for a while. But right then, I knew how completely my heart belonged to him. I remember he asked me something about my height, and I told him he'd grown over the summer.

I'm in love with him, I kept thinking, the whole rest of the night. My whole body had hummed with quiet realization. When I looked over at him in the booth, he seemed to glow. And for the next seven years, I still had moments that felt like echoes of that one.

I loved his focus and intensity when he played piano. I loved the way he cared so deeply about everyone around him, the way he quietly took care of everyone, even if he pretended he didn't. I loved that he just carried facts around inside of him, like which beaches had shipwrecks. I loved how he remembered that Aaron hated pepperoni pizza but that Simon loved it. And I loved the way that he just took me as I was, from the very first moment he met me. I didn't have to try and make myself likable for him. He was that way with everyone—just accepting, with no desire for the people around him to be any different.

Now, walking on the beach beside Felix, I thought to myself, *he's mine and I'm his*. It wasn't possessive exactly, or even really all that romantic. It was a simple declaration of fact. We belonged to each other. I think we had from the moment we met.

I didn't know if we would ever be together in the way I yearned for us to be. But no matter what happened or didn't happen, he was here now, walking beside me. Handing me pennies and telling me about shipwrecks and kissing my temple.

My best friend and the love of my life.

CHAPTER 18

The First Five Don't Count

ROSE

Lying in my bed with Felix, I was so overwhelmed with pleasure and release that I could barely keep my eyes open. But then I thought about what had just happened, and I was wide awake. I couldn't quite get myself to believe it. Even as I was lying with my head on Felix's bare chest, it didn't seem real. I had just had sex with Felix. I had been naked with Felix, and he had kissed my neck and my lips and my boobs, and I'd had an orgasm with him underneath me.

He had had an orgasm underneath me.

Oh my god.

It was like the entire world was rearranged. A world that I wasn't quite sure how to navigate.

"Hey, Felix?" I asked.

"Hmmm?" he replied, his fingers drifting lazily over my skin.

"What now?"

"That's kind of up to you," he said. "This is your thing."

An unexpected ripple of disappointment moved through me.

"Yeah," I said.

I was glad he was giving me control in this situation. But there was a small part of me that wished he was more invested in this for himself. I hadn't fully realized it before, but I think I had some distant daydream that as soon as we had sex, he'd realize how great it was, and want more of it. Want more of *me*.

But that wasn't what we were doing. We were friends. One experienced friend and one inexperienced friend. (Although not quite as inexperienced anymore.) I thought through the options, which were really just to call it or to keep going, at least for a little while. Felix *had* said "ongoing education," and I wasn't ready to let go of it yet.

"I think I kind of want a few more times of this," I replied.

"Well, Wendy always says the first five don't count, so."

I looked up to find him smiling at me. I think I'd seen him smile more in the last few weeks than I usually did in six months.

"Does Wendy really say that?" I asked him.

"He says sex with someone new is like making pancakes. Sometimes the first few are a little imperfect. Still good, though," he added.

"But it takes a few tries to get it down?"

"Exactly."

I laid my head back down on Felix's chest, tracing my finger over his skin. (His bare skin. Under my hand. In my bed.) If the first one was imperfect, I might not survive the next few. I couldn't imagine more pleasure than what I had just felt with him. Although, now that I thought about it, there were a handful of things I still hadn't done, and wanted to try.

And I would get to try them with Felix. If I could talk to my 16-year-old self now, she would not believe me. I felt a small twinge of anxiety. *Don't fall harder*, I thought. *Just let this be what it is.*

"Okay," I said. I sat up and looked down at Felix. I was about to keep talking, but then I saw the way he was looking at me. His eyes moved appreciatively over my body, lingering on my lips, my throat, my breasts. I swallowed hard. "Felix?"

"Hmm?" Felix said, still taking me in.

I wasn't going to be able to concentrate if he was looking at me like that. I grabbed a pillow and held it over my chest, and finally, he met my eyes.

"If we're going to do this, I think we need some boundaries," I said.

"Boundaries sound great," Felix said. He put his hands behind his head and looked at me. "What are you thinking?"

"Actually, hold on," I said. I climbed out of bed and walked to my desk, pulling out a notebook and pen. There was a significant part of me that was aware of the fact that I was completely naked, with Felix in my bed. As soon as I returned to my place, I put the pillow in front of me again.

"You don't have to do that," Felix said.

"Do what?"

"Cover yourself up." He slowly reached out and ran a hand along the top of the pillow, and when I didn't stop him, he pulled it gently away. He ran the tip of one finger over the curve of my breast, then covered it with his whole palm and squeezed.

My breathing sped up, the notebook and pen falling out of my hands. Heat flooded the space between my legs.

If this kept going on, we were never going to get to the… what were we doing? Boundaries. And we had to get to the boundaries. Through some willpower I didn't know I possessed, I grabbed Felix's wrist.

"Wait," I said breathlessly. "I can't think when you're doing that."

Felix gave me a cocky smile and put his hands behind his head again.

I was so in love with him. My eyes moved down his toned torso, over the line of hair on his stomach that led to his cock. His strong thighs…

"Rose?"

I blinked and looked up at Felix, who was raising his eyebrows at me.

Right. Boundaries.

"First," I said. "We don't share details with our bandmates."

Felix stared up at the ceiling for a few long moments, then looked back at me. "I think we should tell them what we're doing, though," he said. "Just in general. I don't want to be dishonest. We all should have learned our lesson with Simon and Marlowe. No secret hookups."

I took a deep breath. "What will we tell them?"

Felix shrugged. "That we're friends with benefits for a while. Not dating, just giving you a summer of love."

I tried not to fall to pieces over his using the word "love."

"Okay," I said. "Honesty. We tell them this is a temporary friends with benefits situation. Can we just keep the details private? I don't want to have to answer a bunch of questions or talk about it all with everyone."

"What happens in Rose's bedroom stays in Rose's bedroom," Felix replied. "Or my bedroom. If you want."

"I want," I said, looking into Felix's green eyes. He met

my gaze, holding it. Our smiles widened together. I suddenly remembered that I was supposed to be writing all of this down and picked up the pen and notebook. Good lord, I had never been more distracted in my life. Every single thing Felix said sent my imagination careening in different directions.

I wrote down:

Boundaries.
1. Tell others the situation, but don't share details.

"Add the not dating part," Felix said. "Just so it's clear to everyone."

Another twinge of disappointment. But I wrote it down.

2. We're not dating.

I looked up at him. I really really didn't want to say the next part, but I knew I had to. For my own sanity. "I think," I said, "that if we're not dating, that we can't act like we're dating."

"What do you mean?" Felix frowned at me.

It was killing me to say this. "Like, no kissing outside of 'bedroom time.' No holding hands. No boyfriend/girlfriend cuddling."

"Have you met me?" Felix said. If I was being honest, I knew this boundary wouldn't be a problem for him. Felix wasn't exactly an affectionate person. We'd known each other for years and we rarely even hugged. The man gave off an undeniable black cat energy, even if he was a softie inside. It was one of the things I loved about him. Even if it made my arms ache with longing all the time.

I wrote:

3. No boyfriend/girlfriend behavior outside of bedroom time

I looked up at him. "Anything else?"

Felix looked at the ceiling thoughtfully again. "I think we should have a time cut off. Like, after three months or something, this is done."

His words knocked the wind out of me for a second. I didn't know why. I'd always known this was temporary. But stamping the expiration date onto it felt like a cruel reminder. I tried to make my voice sound as casual as possible when I replied. "Three months sounds good," I said. I glanced at the calendar on my wall, then wrote:

4. Done by August 12

"Anything else?" I asked.

"If this fucks up anything with Queenscout, or my band, or your band, we stop."

I had a sudden memory of Felix and I in college, Felix sobbing in my arms when Eva broke up with him, when their band Avonswan disintegrated. I'd never seen Felix in that much agony before or since. I couldn't imagine being the cause of that kind of pain.

"I promise," I said.

5. The music comes first

"Now quit writing stuff down and come back here," Felix said.

Every now and then, Felix was adorable. Now was one of those times. I smiled as I set the notebook and pen down, then returned to my place in his arms.

He squeezed me tight, and I melted into him. Had this version of Felix always been here? This affectionate, open, flirtatious person? I wondered for a moment if he was like this with every person he slept with. The thought made me feel strangely envious. I wanted this version of Felix for myself. I wanted every version of Felix for myself.

But I also didn't want to ruin this moment with jealousy. So instead I kissed Felix's neck again and sighed, feeling his skin against mine.

I'm Here
By Rose Devangelo

I dreamt of you last night.
We met in an empty venue,
All faded carpet and dusty lights.
I saw you and reached for you.

I placed my palms on your chest,
and pressed my lips to yours.
You cradled my face.
You said,
"I was waiting for you."
I moved my hands
to wrap my arms
more fully around you
and whispered
"I'm here."

CHAPTER 19

Classic Date Night

FELIX

It had been four days since Rose and I slept together. And I had been trying really hard not to replay every second of it in my head since then. I was laying in my bed, listening to Tom Waits' *Bad As Me* album, and failing at not thinking about sex with Rose.

Why had it been so good? There wasn't any wild technique being used or anything. It had to be because we knew each other so well. Because even with Eva, it hadn't felt—

I shook my head to clear that thought away. Eva was in the past, and so was the hurt from dating her, even though I still carried the lessons with me. Specifically that romance was not for me. No sunset walks or lingering eye contact while "making love" or sipping a milkshake with two straws across from some girl. I had nothing against romantic love in principle, I just knew that romance was water and I was oil. Or fire. Or something that didn't mix with water.

Tom Waits sang about there being something comforting in knowing what to expect, and I narrowed my eyes at the record player.

My phone dinged and I glanced down at it. A message from Rose.

> ROSE: Hey wanna go see 'The Blank' with me tonight at 8:50?

A little happy zing moved through my body. Which… weird. Rose and I went to the movies together all the time. We had for years. This was no different. I ignored the unfamiliar butterflies in my stomach and typed out my reply.

> ME: Only if we can eat at Ole's first

> ROSE: Meet you there at 7:30

I glanced at the clock. About half an hour from now, so that worked out. Wait. I frowned, then typed out another message

> ME: The Blank? I thought you hated scary movies

> ROSE: I'm trying new things

Good for her.

Ole's was the best waffle house in Alameda, and Rose and I had both been going there since we were teenagers. It was within walking distance, and it was just a few blocks away from the movie theatre. When I got there, I slid into a booth and waited for Rose to arrive.

When the door opened and she stepped inside, my breath caught for a second. She looked…honestly, the word that came to mind was "lovely." Soft and sweet and good. And beautiful. Maybe it was because I had seen her naked, but she looked amazing. She was wearing this sleeveless dress with sunflowers all over it, and these sandals that made her legs look great, and her short hair was messy in the most perfect way.

She caught my eye and gave me a warm smile.

"Hey," she said, settling into the seat opposite me. We each ordered our usuals—a burger for me, waffles with pecans and caramel for her. When the waitress brought our food out, I frowned. "That always smells so good."

"Well, it has nuts in it, so I'm really sorry, but you can't have any."

"Fucking nut allergy," I grumbled. "Maybe it won't kill me? I haven't tried pecans in years."

"I don't want you to risk your life in an experiment."

"Just a bite," I wheedled.

"If you eat a bite of this," Rose replied, "I'm calling 911 and then your emergency contact."

I scowled and ate a handful of fries from my own plate.

"*You're* my emergency contact," I said. "You and my mom."

Rose blinked at me. "I'm your emergency contact?"

I shrugged. "Who else would I put?"

She gave her head a small shake. Then she smiled at me. "It's just that you're mine," she said.

I raised my eyebrows at her. "Not Jem?"

"I've known you longer."

Satisfaction swelled in my chest. I didn't know why that made me feel so goddamn good. Knowing Rose trusted me like that made me feel strong and protective and a bunch of other patriarchal bullshit that I didn't believe in. But it also made me feel like…like I belonged to Rose. Like I was a permanent fixture in her life, and she was one in mine. I didn't have that with many people.

It's because you love her as a friend, I told myself. Which was true.

THE MOVIE WAS BOTH REALLY stupid and actually kind of scary. A complete rip-off of (not homage to) another block-buster horror movie from last summer. At the first jump-scare, Rose yelped and grabbed my arm, clinging to me like she was holding on for dear life. She didn't let go, and over the next twenty minutes, her grip on my arm grew tighter. When I glanced over at her, her eyes were wide with fright. She seemed legitimately terrified.

And I was discovering that I actually hated to see her scared like this?

"Jesus, Rose," I whispered. I tried to free my arm, but she wouldn't let me. "I'm trying to put my arm around you," I said.

Rose remained staring at the screen, but she loosened her grip enough for me to lift my arm and pull her into me. When a demon onscreen crawled out from under a bed, she buried her face in my chest.

She was killing me here. This was stupid. Why did I have the insane urge to *protect* her?! From a *movie*? Like I was some sort of conservative boy from the 1950s or a goddamn caveman or something.

"We don't have to stay," I whispered into her hair.

"I'm being brave," she replied, her voice muffled.

"You're not even watching the movie," I pointed out.

"I'm being brave with my ears."

I chuckled drily and shook my head. This sweet girl. I

had the sudden urge to kiss the top of her head. But Rose said no boyfriend/girlfriend stuff outside of the bedroom, so I resisted.

"Well, if you want to leave," I said, "we can leave."

We didn't leave, but stayed until the credits, at which point Rose was brave enough to lift her head and look at me.

"I don't think I like scary movies."

I threw my hands up. "I know you don't like scary movies! Why the shit did we see this movie?"

Rose looked at the screen and sighed. "Apparently, not all of the new things I try are worth it."

I had a sudden, horrible thought. "Rose," I said. "Were you scared to have sex?"

Her eyes darted over to me, and she shook her head. "No. No no no no no, not at *all*. Why?"

I breathed a sigh of relief. "Because seeing this movie scared you but you did it anyway."

"Not *all* new things are scary," Rose said. "Or at least, they don't have to be. Or they can be worth it. Like, even if you're scared you can do it anyway and it's worth it."

I nodded. Something about what Rose just said was pinging something in my chest, but I didn't feel like investigating it. "Speaking of scary," I said, "I'm walking you home." I stood up, and in another weird moment, I had the instinct to offer Rose my hand. I stuffed both hands into my pockets to stifle the urge.

We walked north toward her house in silence for a few moments. When I stole a glance at her, she had her arms wrapped around herself, goosebumps on her skin.

Fuck it, this was stupid. I pulled off my jacket and draped it over her shoulders. She smiled at me gratefully, and a few minutes later, she let out a small laugh.

"What?" I asked.

She looked at me for a moment, as if weighing whether or not to speak. She faced forward again as she said, "It just occurred to me that we just had a classic date night. Dinner and a movie. And now you're walking me home."

Something in my gut lurched. "We've done this literally a hundred times before," I said. "Probably more."

Rose shrugged. "I know," she said. "It just felt a little different tonight. Considering…everything."

"But we're not dating," I said. It came out way douche-ier than I meant it to, but it was true.

"I know," Rose said.

Fuck, it did feel like a date, though. It had the whole time. I don't think I would have recognized it if Rose hadn't said anything, but now the weight of it was making my heart pound.

When we got to her place, Rose pulled my jacket off her shoulders and handed it to me.

"Thanks," I said, shrugging it back on. She stood across from me, and without thinking about it, my gaze dropped down to her lips.

They looked soft and pillowy. Warm and inviting. She was such a good kisser.

"Felix?" Rose asked quietly.

"Yeah?" I knew I should probably stop looking at her mouth, but I was having a hard time tearing my eyes away.

"I know we're not dating," she said. "But I feel like this is the part of the date when you're supposed to kiss me goodnight."

Fuck. I swallowed. *Don't let this get away from you*, I thought.

"We're not in your bedroom," I replied. "Or we're not —this isn't practice time. Or whatever. That was one of the boundaries, right?"

"I wasn't asking you to kiss me." I couldn't tell if there was a hint of disappointment in Rose's voice or not.

We stood in silence for a moment.

"Right," I said. "Okay. Well. See you at the show tomorrow."

I turned and walked into the night, not waiting for Rose to reply.

CHAPTER 20

Two Straws

FELIX

"Hey Mar, where's my guitar?" Simon asked, frowning. He stood up from where he was sitting on the edge of the stage.

Marlowe frowned back at him, setting her own guitar case down on the ground. "I don't know where your guitar is," she said. She turned to go get the rest of her gear.

"I asked you to bring it," Simon called after her.

She turned. "And I told you I didn't have room in my car."

"When did you say that?"

"When you asked me to bring your guitar."

Simon growled in frustration, and my shoulders tensed in response. "So it's just back at my place?"

"Must be," Marlowe shrugged, before walking out the back door. The tension she left behind made the air feel heavy.

"Goddammit," Simon grumbled.

The whole room felt tense with their fight. Fuck shit damn. I hated this. Why why why did we think it would work to have people in our bands dating?

When Marlowe got back inside, she started setting up her pedal board and amp, not really acknowledging Simon pacing nearby. "I don't know how the fuck our wires got crossed here," he started. "But now I have to go all the way back to Alameda to grab my stuff."

"I'm not your fucking roadie, Simon," Marlowe said, not looking up from what she was doing.

"I didn't say you were! I would have asked one of the guys to grab my gear but I was already texting you this morning from here!"

The rest of us were silently setting up our own gear. With every second that Simon and Marlowe kept arguing, my blood pressure went up ten points. Sure, sometimes we all got annoyed with each other as bandmates, or disagreed about something. Aaron and Wendy never did their goddamn dishes at home. Simon and I sometimes fought about lyrics. None of us could agree on the best venue. But this shit between Simon and Marlowe was exactly why the Oregon Rule was created. Because things got messy when people were dating. I didn't want us all to play like shit because Simon and Marlowe were in some kind of lover's spat.

Finally, Simon stomped out to go get his guitar. Aaron watched him go, frowning. Wendy seemed extra focused on pulling his cymbals out, while Jem and Marlowe were both actively ignoring everyone else. Rose looked genuinely worried, and *that* pissed me off.

"So is sound check just fucked then?" I asked.

"We can still run sound check with the rest of us," Aaron said calmly, turning to me. "And we can add

Simon's vocals and guitar to the mix right before the show?" He turned to the sound guy. "Does that work, Tori?"

Tori gave us a thumbs up.

"Fine," I said. "Start with whoever's ready."

I was finishing setting up my keyboard when I felt a gentle hand on my arm. I looked up to see Rose standing nearby. I took in her tender eyes, her soft touch.

"You okay?" she asked quietly.

"Fuckin' great," I replied, turning back to my keyboard. "Just fantastic."

"It'll be okay, Felix," Rose whispered.

"Sure fuckin' hope so," I muttered, shaking my head. I watched as Rose went back to pick up her bass for sound check.

I closed my eyes. She didn't deserve that. Why the hell was I such a dick *all* of the time? Rose was just trying to be kind, and I was being such a grouch. I hadn't exactly said anything mean *to* Rose, but I could feel that I was armed with darts ready to throw at anyone who came too close.

We finished sound check and then Jem and I sat down to come up with the set list, and I wasn't in any better of a mood an hour and a half later when Simon came back. He and Marlowe were *noticeably* not talking to each other as he set up.

I was ready for this to be the worst show we'd ever played.

OUR FIRST SONG did genuinely suck. Tori was still trying to set levels, and Simon hadn't finished setting up his pedal board and his guitar got unplugged halfway through. Our second song wasn't much better, and I was preparing for us to bomb the rest of the night. And I was furious about it.

But then Marlowe and Jem stepped up to sing "Aqua Tofana," and it was like all of their rage was being funneled into the words. Especially Marlowe's. It was feminism rage plus annoyed girlfriend rage.

And it was powerful.

Not so powerful that I thought Marlowe and Simon *should* get into a fight before every show, but powerful enough that maybe it was working out what she needed to work out. Marlowe whipped her hair around as she strode across the stage, stopping on the edge to head bang with the audience. Jem moved violently as she sang, stomping fiercely to the beat. The rest of us had to turn up our own performances to match theirs. And somehow I found my own rage and fear being funneled out of me, out of my fingers, into the keys, into the music. All of us were breathless when we hit the last chord.

I looked over to see Marlowe and Simon staring at each other, Marlowe's chest heaving. Finally, she gave him a small nod, and he returned it.

By the time we got to "Roadside Motel," the tension had dissipated some. But I still felt like I was waiting for aftershocks. Like the danger wasn't totally past.

We finished out the show, and I was quiet as I packed up, but I saw Marlowe and Simon talking quietly in a corner. When we all got out to the parking lot, they stopped us.

"Okay," Simon said. "Marlowe and I are buying everyone milkshakes."

"Sorry we were both dicks to you guys," Marlowe said.

For some reason, everyone turned to look at me. I raised my eyebrows. Maybe it was because the Oregon Rule was my rule, or because I was the co-leader of our band. Or maybe because I was the most noticeably bothered by everything that had gone on tonight. But I didn't want to dwell on it.

"Fine," I said, nodding quickly. "I don't care if you guys fight, just don't bring it to shows or practice."

Which wasn't totally true—I did actually care if they fought, and I couldn't imagine them fighting and not taking it to shows or practice. But there was no way I could possibly tell them what to do as a couple.

"Scout's honor," Simon said.

I rolled my eyes. "Floyd's?" I asked.

"Floyd's," Marlowe replied. It was an ice cream shop a few blocks away. We ended up there half the time we had gigs at this venue anyway.

When we walked inside, Rose sidled up next to me. She squeezed my hand once and then let go.

How did she do that? Rearrange my spine so that it was in the right place again? Just by like, *existing*? I seemed to set everyone on edge just by existing.

I leaned down. "Thanks," I whispered into her hair.

She smiled up at me. The sweetest girl on the planet, who kissed with so much passion and loved so fiercely. My arms literally ached to hold her in this moment. I wanted to pull her into me, rest my chin on the top of her head. I wanted to keep her in my arms while we stood in line, so that when it was her turn to order, she would have to turn around and press her back against my chest. I imagined pressing my hips into the soft curve of her back, right above her ass. My arms could come around her waist. Then later, in her bedroom, I could pull off her clothes, kiss my way down her torso...

"Want to share a milkshake?" Rose asked.

I blinked at her, her words forcing me back into the

moment. I shoved my hands into my pockets, and tried to process what Rose had just said. "What?" I asked.

"Do you want to share a milkshake?"

I suppressed a laugh. Wasn't this the exact scenario I had pushed away from my mind the other night? On our non-date date? Rose's brown eyes smiled at me.

Fuck it. One milkshake, two straws. Whatever.

CHAPTER 21

We Didn't Fall

ROSE

I didn't know how Ducky convinced us all to do this. This was insane. We were supposed to be on tour along the Oregon and California coast, not doing "team building activities" that might kill us. Treetop Adventures was an "elevated ropes course," but all I could see was a hundred different ways we could die. Or be seriously injured. The helmets and harnesses were not making me feel any safer. Neither was the waiver we had all just signed.

Our first task was to simply climb a tree using the handholds until we got to the platform on top. From the looks of it, we were then supposed to walk on a few ropes to another platform, like we were circus performers or something.

A few minutes ago, Aaron asked how all of this was legal, and I was wondering the same thing. Still, he didn't even hesitate as he pulled himself up to the platform, thirty feet above us. I watched as Wendy made it halfway up, when his foot slipped. He came racing toward the ground, and I screamed and closed my eyes. But when I opened them, it was to find that Wendy had landed safely in a crouch, the ropes and harnesses keeping him from getting hurt. He laughed and started climbing again.

I was having trouble breathing.

Wendy joined Aaron safely at the top, and then Jem gritted her teeth and followed after them.

And then it was my turn.

My fingers shook as I reached up to grab the first handhold. My stomach was churning with terror. I closed my eyes and tried to just breathe for a moment. What I really wanted was to turn around and bury myself in Felix's arms and have him tell me it was all okay. But Felix and I's friendship didn't really include long comforting hugs unless there was an emergency.

You can do this, I thought to myself. *It's just like being up in the catwalks of a theatre.*

That thought gave me some courage. I'd spent hours at much higher heights than this, without a harness, hanging speakers and plugging in cables. Of course, there had been railings then, but the harness would catch me if I fell.

My hands still shook, but I pulled myself up anyway. I took one step up, then another, and then I was there at the platform, and Jem was nodding at me.

I couldn't bring myself to look down over the edge of the platform, but I could hear Felix cursing below. It kind of went on for a while before he yelled "Fuck it!" And thirty seconds later, he was there on the platform next to me, looking a little shaken but trying to hide it.

It seemed like Ducky was on the platform two seconds later, because she was insane and must have sprinted up right after Felix. When it was Marlowe's turn, I brought myself to peer over the edge at the ground. My stomach lurched.

Okay, I thought. *Okay*. We were at least thirty feet in the air. I gave the rope attached to my harness a gentle tug, to make sure I was still secured to the tree. It felt reassuringly strong. I forced myself to watch Simon climb up after Marlowe, and then we were all there, none of us dead or injured. Yet.

I had hardly managed to process the climb we'd all just done when the guide started explaining the next part of the ropes course. There was a "bridge" of five or six ropes all strung lengthwise from this platform to the next, and apparently we were supposed to cross it in pairs. There was another rope strung above the bridge as a hand hold.

"You can try any method of getting across you want," the guide said. "But if one of you falls, you both fall. So pick someone you either trust or want to trust."

Jem grabbed Ducky's hand, and I immediately turned my eyes to Felix. I took a step closer to him right as he stepped closer to me. It gave me a tiny bit of relief to know we were about to do this together.

Ducky was being her usual fearless, reckless self, and I watched her run out onto the ropes, towing Jem violently behind her. It seemed like she was trying to use speed to get across. But it wasn't enough. They plummeted toward the ground, Jem screaming and Ducky laughing.

I turned to Felix's frowning face. "How are we going to do this?" I asked.

He folded his arms and looked out at the ropes. "Crouch," he said. "Hold on to the ropes and each other."

"What?" I asked. I was busy staring out at the ropes and couldn't quite comprehend what he was suggesting.

The guide started clipping Felix in to the next part of

the course, and then clipping me to the same line, and then clipping us together.

"Like this," Felix said. He clapped a hand onto my shoulder and forced us both into a crouch. He gripped the ropes below us with his other hand. Then he turned his intense green eyes to me. I nodded and mirrored his pose, placing one hand on the ropes below us and one on his shoulder.

And then we stepped sideways off of the platform.

I could feel Felix's breath on my face. The scent of him washed over me, the same familiar spice I'd come to know and love, and my eyes fell closed. I was sure that the grip of Felix's hand on my shoulder was going to leave a bruise. I was clinging to his shoulder just as tightly. We were hardly ever this close. It was almost too much.

"Rose, you have to open your eyes," Felix gritted out.

When I did, it was to see his face inches from mine. His piercing gaze almost made me more dizzy than the heights did.

He nodded at me.

And we started moving. After a few feet, I found that I could sort of pull myself along with my grip on the ropes. It was slow, unsteady work. I couldn't hold Felix's gaze for very long, so I focused instead on my hand on the ropes.

I turned to check our progress. We were halfway there.

"Dick fuck this is shitting scary as hell," Felix grumbled, his voice a little shaky.

Even though I was so scared that I could hardly think straight, I smiled. One of my favorite things about Felix had always been his creative swearing.

"Just—keep—going," I said. My own voice was trembling so much I could barely get the words out.

I saw Felix nod once, a curt movement of his head. He

was gritting his teeth so hard I could see veins in his neck starting to bulge.

Just a few more feet. Maybe we could actually do this!

I chose that moment to glance down, and suddenly felt faint. I swayed a little.

Felix's grip on my shoulder tightened. "We're almost there, Rose," Felix said.

I looked into his face, so open and honest, and suddenly everything in me went still. He was here. Felix was here with me, and we were doing this together, and no matter what else ever did or didn't happen between us, he was here right now. I could trust him to catch me, hold me steady. Pull me across when the depths threatened to pull me down. I took a deep breath and nodded at him.

Our knees knocked together a few times as we got closer to the platform. But the ropes beneath us felt steadier too. Almost there…

I collapsed onto the platform, and felt Felix do the same thing next to me. I turned to him. He was grinning wildly at me, and it was so rare and bright and wonderful that I couldn't help but return it.

"We didn't fall," Felix said.

"We didn't fall," I repeated.

He sat up. "And thank god," he said. "If you had fallen, I would have fallen with you."

I sat up and nodded. Something about that phrasing made my insides feel a little strange.

"I would have caught you," I said.

"I know," Felix replied. He stood and offered me his hand. I took it and let him haul me up. "You always catch me," he added.

I wanted to tell him everything right then. To let the words pour out of me, to say how all I ever wanted to do for the rest of my life was to catch him, and to let myself be caught by him. How I loved the ridiculous way he swore and the way his hair was sticking out from under his helmet right now and the way his hands looked when he played piano. I wanted to tell him that my heart was his.

But I couldn't. Not while we were surrounded by our friends, and on tour together with our bands. So instead, I just smiled at him and said, "You always catch me, too."

CHAPTER 22

Because I Wanted To

FELIX

When I got to Rose's room, it was to find her laying on the floor, scrolling her phone, her head toward me.

"Hey," I said.

She tilted her head back to look at me. Even upside down like this, her smile was still cute.

"I was looking up the liner notes," she said.

I shut her door and laid down beside her. "I miss CDs," I sighed.

"You're not old enough to miss CDs," Rose replied, smiling.

"We both know I'm like eighty years old on the inside." I frowned. "Speaking of which, why the fuck are we laying on your floor?"

"Because we always lay on the floor when listening to new albums," Rose replied. "We have since we were teenagers."

I sat up and looked down at her. Shit damn, she looked

pretty. I had noticed Rose's perfect lips more in the last month than I ever had for our entire friendship. "Yeah, but we're grownups now. Let's lay in the *bed*."

Rose looked at me for a long moment, then sat up. Once we were settled side by side on her mattress, she pressed play on her phone and let Stonewallflower's most recent album start playing over her bluetooth speaker.

I closed my eyes. This album was softer than their previous one. I followed the melody as it meandered quietly, like it was walking through the woods.

This was my favorite way to experience new music. Laying next to Rose, just focusing on each track, letting it wash over us. The first time we did this was only a few months after we met, and we'd been listening to new albums together like this ever since.

The second song on the album was bigger, more dramatic. It felt old and yearning, like some kind of British gothic novel. I could practically hear the wind rushing over the moors. I'd always wanted to write songs like this— maybe I could, in a few years.

When the song ended, Rose paused the album and turned to me. "That song felt like Wuthering Heights," she said. I looked over.

"I was literally thinking the same thing," I replied.

A slow smile spread over Rose's face. Everything about Rose was so soft. Her eyes, her smile. The words she used. The way her skin felt. Damn, there were so many things about her that I liked. I felt my heart speed up slightly, and then I watched her eyes dip down to my mouth.

And then, because I could, because I wanted to, I closed the distance between us and kissed her.

It was gentle at first. Her lips moved tenderly against mine, her hands cupping my jaw softly.

Goddamn *fuck*, how had I forgotten how good it felt to

kiss Rose?! I parted my lips and felt her gasp quietly, and I leaned into her more, chasing that gasp. I felt her soft tongue lick into my mouth.

Holy goddamn shit.

Heat rushed through my entire body, making me suddenly ravenous. I tilted my head, deepening our kiss, feeling her melt into me. We were going from zero to sixty in like, three seconds, but it felt way too good for me to care.

I let my hand skim over Rose's waist, then slip under her t-shirt, moving slowly up until I was cupping one of her tits over her lace bralette. Her tits were so *perfect*. When I squeezed, Rose let out one of those breathy moans that went straight to my cock.

My hips rolled, seeking friction. My hardness rubbed up against Rose's thigh, aching, wanting. Then the heel of her hand was there, moving up and down, palming me through my pants. I stifled a moan.

Her fingers slowly undid my top button, then slid the zipper down. I opened my eyes to see Rose looking intently at me. Then she turned her attention back to my cock. She pulled it out of my briefs, then sat up and swung a leg over me, so that she was straddling my thighs.

She squeezed my hardness gently, then slid her hand up and down my length. My teeth clenched with the torturous pleasure of it.

"Show me," she whispered. I looked up at her, her cheeks flushed, her nipples pointed beneath her shirt.

I reached out and brought her hand to my mouth. I let my tongue glide from her wrist, over her palm, along her fingers, until her skin was wet. Then I guided her hand back down to my cock.

I slowly wrapped one of my hands around hers, so that we were both grasping my hardness, her small soft hand beneath mine. I moved our hands slowly up and down, showing her the pressure that I liked.

After a few slow, intense minutes, Rose let go of me and scooted herself farther down. She gave me an inquisitive look. Then she lowered her mouth and slowly, so slowly, let her lips envelop the tip of my cock.

I was going to die. Fucking shit, her perfect warm mouth felt so good. Then she swirled her tongue over me and I swear I blacked out for a second. I heard myself make a strangled cry.

Rose sat up suddenly. "Was that okay?"

I looked up at her worried expression. "Rose, that was fucking amazing."

"I don't know how to…how…tell me what feels good," Rose said.

"What you just did felt fucking great," I replied.

Rose smiled, then reached out and ran a finger from the tip of my dick to the base. She was killing me. "I want more guidance," she said shyly.

"This is going to sound dumb," I replied, breathless. "But treat it like a popsicle."

Rose giggled, her eyebrows raised. Then she lowered her head and pressed her tongue against my shaft, licking slowly up. Then she did it again. And again. Then she pulled the tip of me into her mouth and sucked.

I was gripping the bedsheets so tightly that I thought I might rip them. The muscles of my thighs were clenching, my body getting dangerously closer to release. I was clinging to control with every ounce of willpower I had, trying not to thrust up into Rose's mouth, trying not to spill into her. Everything in me was tightening, but I didn't want this to end yet. I wanted more of her. I wanted to know how to make *her* feel this good. I reached down to grip her shoulders.

"Rose, wait," I managed.

She sat up and looked at me with concern. "Is every-thing okay?" she asked. "Did I…?"

"Rose, oh my fucking god Rose, that felt so good that I was about to…Jesus, Rose." It was the closest I could get to an explanation, apparently.

The grin she flashed me was sudden, white-hot. She reached out for me again.

"Wait!" I said. She paused, looking at me uncertainly. "I just want…I want to know what makes *you* feel good." When she didn't respond, I added, "I promise that you going down on me was incredible. Fucking damn hell, it felt good, Rose, and we can definitely do it again. But I want…" I trailed off at the sight of Rose's frown.

It suddenly became really important for her to know this. I sat up and cupped her face with my hands. "Rose. I want to know how to coax pleasure out of *your* body. I want to make you sigh and moan and grip the sheets like I was a second ago. I want to know how to make you come."

Rose's mouth had fallen open at some point, and now she was staring at me. "You…you made me come last time?" she offered. "With…sex." But I shook my head.

"The first few don't count," I replied. "Tell me how to make you come *consistently*."

Rose covered her face with her hands and shook her head. "This is embarrassing," she said, her voice slightly muffled. "I don't know how to tell you."

I pulled her hands away from her face. "Then show me," I said. I had no idea when this had switched from Rose's education to mine, but I needed to know. Rose studied my face. "Show me how you touch yourself."

I watched as one emotion after another moved over Rose's face. Uncertainty, arousal, anxiety. "It's me, Rose," I whispered.

Her face softened slightly, then I saw a determined heat in her eyes. She moved off of me, and then slipped her shorts and underwear off. She laid back against the pillows, and I watched as her hand slowly moved down her chest to rest between her legs.

Wait. Holy shit. I hadn't realized how hot this would be. I was honestly just wanting to learn, but now Rose was bare from the waist down, and she was looking straight into my eyes as her fingers began to move.

There was not enough air in the room, but I wouldn't leave it even if someone tried to drag me out. All I could do was scoot to the edge of the bed so that I was directly across from Rose. I watched as two of her fingers circled her clit, smaller circles and bigger circles, her chest moving up and down with more and more speed.

I reached out to wrap a hand around one of her ankles, my cock twitching. I needed something to anchor myself, keep me upright while this perfect girl was touching herself.

CHAPTER 23

Good Isn't a Strong Enough Word For It

ROSE

The way Felix was looking at me was making me feel hot and seen and bare. For a few moments, it was hard to concentrate, hard to move my fingers the way I usually did, with his eyes on me. When he had grabbed my ankle, it had sent electricity right through me. But soon my hands found a rhythm again, and I felt myself winding tighter, moving higher.

I paused. "I usually…" I didn't know how to finish the sentence I had started.

"Tell me," Felix said, his voice tight, his hand palming himself.

I remembered the way he had told me to just say things, without worrying about sounding "sexy" or whatever. "I usually get out the vibrator. At this point," I said quietly.

Felix's throat bobbed up and down as he swallowed. "Do you want to use it now?"

"Should I?" I asked. "Is that like, bad sex manners or something? I don't want you to feel—"

"Rose," Felix said. He laid a hand on my thigh. "The vibrator and I are on the same team." I giggled. "We are both Team Get Rose Off," Felix continued. "You don't have to use your vibrator if you don't want to right now, but if you want to show me, I would sure as shit like to see."

I searched his face, his green eyes looking intense and lustful. But there was a softness there, too. A tenderness I could trust. I reached over to my nightstand.

It was nothing fancy, just a small wand. But I turned it on and then looked into Felix's face as I pressed it between my legs. I gasped with the pleasure of it.

Felix was breathing heavily, watching me. His pants were still slung down around his hips, revealing how turned on he still was. I wanted to see all of him, the long lines of him.

"Take your clothes off," I gasped.

Felix whipped his shirt over his head, and stood long enough to shove his pants and briefs all the way down. I paused my own movements to pull my shirt and bralette off. When he was naked, Felix knelt at the end of my bed, almost between my feet. His black hair fell into his green eyes, and his jaw tightened as one hand wrapped around his cock.

His gaze dropped between my legs as I began moving the wand against myself again. I felt desperate, hungrily chasing my own pleasure. I wanted Felix to be even more of a part of it. I had a sudden vision of my hands buried in his hair, my legs flung over his shoulders, the way so many of my books had described. The thought made me catch my breath. I let my hand fall still.

"Why did you stop?" Felix asked.

I swallowed. "Because I want…" The words felt slightly foreign, but I said them anyway. "I want you to go down on me."

Felix didn't even pause. He backed off the edge of the bed, dropped to his knees, and yanked my legs toward him. My thighs were on either side of his head before I could even get my bearings. Then he plunged his mouth into the core of me, and I gasped.

It wasn't like anything I'd ever felt before. The surprising heat of Felix's tongue between my legs was so unfamiliar, so delicious, that I reached behind my head to grasp my pillow, my back arching.

Felix swirled his tongue in a circle, first larger, then smaller. It was exactly what I needed. I bit my lip to keep from crying out too loudly. After a few moments, I realized that he was mimicking what he'd seen me do with my own fingers.

I reached down with one hand to grasp at his hair. "F…F…Felix…" I whimpered.

Hearing my strangled words seemed to do something to him—his hands squeezed my thighs tighter and he made a muffled moaning sound. But kept the same rhythm with his mouth.

When I had daydreamed about this, a boy's lips between my legs, I had always worried that I would be self-conscious. That I would get caught up thinking about how I tasted or smelled, or if the other person was actually enjoying themselves. But right now I was too caught up in pleasure for any of those thoughts to even enter my brain.

Felix's tongue was sending me higher and higher, bringing me closer to my climax. One of my hands clutched at his hair while the other clung to the pillow my head was resting on. I felt my hips tilt once, twice, and then my orgasm came crashing through me, undulating waves of pleasure, spinning around the tight spot where Felix's mouth remained pinned.

Finally, I collapsed back onto the bed, my legs dangling over Felix's shoulders. After a few moments, he gently lifted my thighs and climbed back onto the bed. I looked up to see him grinning at me, his lips and chin slick with my arousal. Maybe I might have felt embarrassed about that, but I was too blinded by my orgasm and Felix's smile to care.

"That was…" My chest was still heaving. "I feel…"

"Good," Felix said. It was both the completion of my sentence and his response to it. He reached for a tissue beside my bed and wiped his face. Somehow the sight of *that* was also attractive?

"'Good' isn't a strong enough word for it," I said. Felix collapsed beside me, running a finger gently down my neck.

"Eating women out is one of my favorite things, honestly," Felix said. I felt a tiny lurch in my center. That simple sentence reminded me that Felix was so much more experienced than I was. I was definitely getting the benefit of that right now, but it also meant that there had been other women he'd done this with. The thought made me feel sort of left behind. There was a loneliness to the knowledge that Felix had done more, with people that weren't me.

"Hey," Felix said softly.

To my embarrassment, tears filled my eyes.

"Hey, are you okay?" Felix asked, genuine concern in his voice.

I nodded, blinking rapidly. "Yeah," I said quietly.

Felix just waited, knowing I would tell him what I was thinking when I was ready to, if I wanted to.

"I feel…" I started. I took a breath. "I'm just so aware

of how much more experienced you are. Like, all of these things are firsts for me, and that makes them feel like a really big deal, but you've already done them, so they're not a big deal for you, and it makes me feel… 'left out' isn't the right word, but something like it."

I could feel all of my other, deeper feelings churning around beneath my words. The implication that this was more meaningful for me was so closely attached to what I felt for Felix that what I said took on a tinge of confession.

"It's a big deal for me," Felix whispered.

I whipped my head to the side, staring at him. He was looking up at the ceiling, his face guarded.

"What do you mean?" I asked. My heart was pounding. I could barely bring myself to hope the impossible, that he loved me the same way I loved him, that he was falling for me, that all of this had awoken something in him. I could barely breathe.

Felix shrugged. "I just mean that it's a big deal to me to be your first," he said. He turned to look at me. "You mean a lot to me, Rose. I'm glad you chose me for this. I think I would have been upset if it had been someone else, actually."

My thoughts were tumbling around so quickly that I felt disoriented. There was no confession, but those words about me meaning a lot to him were so matter-of-fact, such a simple statement of truth, that they filled my chest with warmth. The fact that he wanted to be my first was so surprising, so tender, that I didn't know what to say.

So I didn't say anything. I leaned forward and kissed him, pressing my lips to his slowly and deliberately. I placed a hand on his chest and leaned into the kiss, feeling him reach up into my hair, turn his body toward me.

Felix opened his mouth and soon we were both breathing quickly again. His body was rolling against mine, his breath coming in throaty gasps. He kissed me all over—my lips, my collarbones, my eyelids. He whispered my name against the sensitive spot below my ear. His hands moved over my body as if he were painting it, lingering when my breath hitched. I was drowning in the goodness of it.

I watched Felix roll a condom on. He cupped one side of my face, looking into my eyes while he pushed himself inside of me.

Everything about it felt so *right*. He filled me up so perfectly. His skin against mine made me feel at home in my own body in a way that nothing else ever had.

We moved together slowly, Felix bracing himself with one arm above me. My fingers splayed over his chest, feeling the push and retreat of him. Heat and pleasure gathered in my center again, and I lifted my legs to wrap them around Felix. This man I had known and loved for so long, whose touch was growing familiar to me.

When he felt my heels dig into his lower back, he started to move faster, and I brought my hands around his torso, pulling him closer to me with each forward movement.

"Felix," I whispered. He looked down and held my gaze, his green eyes looking deep into mine.

He whispered my name back. His thrusts were getting sharper, and in two more breaths, I was crying out, another orgasm rushing through me. Felix pressed his forehead against mine, and I felt his own release pulsing, as our bodies fitted together, as we gasped into each other's mouths.

CHAPTER 24

Cool Down, Boy

FELIX

This is what it's supposed to be, I thought. Rose and I, naked and trembling, our bodies heaving with connection and pleasure. I buried my forehead in her shoulder as I came down from my climax. I wanted to breathe with her, chest to chest, until our breathing slowed. I wanted to wrap myself around her, let her curl her body into mine, tangle our limbs together until sleep took us both.

I wanted it so much that it scared the shit out of me.

When Rose spoke, I could hear the smile in her voice. "We'll have to re-listen to this Stonewallflower album again," she said.

I slowly became aware of the music still playing. How had I not noticed there was music playing? I *always* noticed when there was music playing. I lifted my head and looked down into Rose's warm brown eyes, her soft smile warming every part of me.

Shit fuck damn shit fuck.

It was happening.

No, it had already *happened*.

I was catching feelings. My chest tightened with panic at the thought, my stomach dropping. It suddenly felt like my skin was on fire.

I was risking every single good thing I had by developing a goddamn *crush*. My friendship with Rose, our bands, the entire "friends with benefits for educational purposes" thing. All of it was going to crumble because I couldn't keep my shit together. I had to get out of here.

I pulled away from Rose and got rid of the condom. "Hey, sorry, I just remembered," I said. "I have a thing today." I pulled my briefs and pants on, not looking at her.

"Do you have to go?" Rose asked. There was a note of longing in her voice that went right through me, leaving me feeling all achey. I still couldn't meet her eyes.

"Yeah, sorry," I said, yanking my shirt over my head.

"That's okay," Rose replied. "We can find another time to listen to the album."

"Yeah. See ya."

If Rose had expected me to kiss her goodbye, I didn't take the time to notice. I left her room without looking at her.

I started the walk home, my thoughts churning. This had never happened to me before. So I guess I didn't know if I was "catching feelings" exactly. By the time Eva and I were hooking up, my feelings were already caught. And I always shut anything else down with other people before it started.

What Rose and I had just done, that hadn't felt like friends with benefits. Almost none of it even felt "educational." I kissed her because I wanted to. It was the kind of spontaneous sex that I imagined couples have. I couldn't believe I was *feeling* things. But the insane part, the part that had my insides doing somersaults, was that none of the things I felt seemed exactly new. It all just felt deeper.

Fuck, I'd practically confessed it, too. Telling her that she meant a lot to me, that I would have been upset if she had chosen someone else to do this with.

The whole walk home, I could feel my heart hammering in my chest. I felt like something was chasing me, and I spent longer than was reasonable trying to resist the physical urge to break into a run.

I needed something—music, a drive, video games. Something to get me out of my head.

Out of my heart.

Because I knew how this would end. It would end with Rose giving me a sympathetic frown and explaining that this was all casual and then I would spend a day crying in someone's arms.

Or crying alone because I would lose Rose's arms.

Panic squeezed my chest. I couldn't lose Rose. I couldn't.

When I got home, I ignored the other guys and went straight to my room. I pulled the cover off my keyboard and sat down, immediately letting some bluesy chords spill out of me. I didn't sing in front of audiences, really, but it was how I wrote songs. And it was also sometimes how I figured out what to do about shit that was messing with my head. I let the words come to me as my hands moved over the keys.

> *Cool down, boy*
> *You're just a passenger*
> *She said she's gonna drive*

> *And you said you'd ride with her*
> *Just keep your seatbelt on*
> *And your eyes looking ahead*
> *Don't let things get too tangled*
> *In the sheets of her bed*

I sat back.

According to the words I had just written, I was apparently *not* going to end this thing with Rose? It sounded like my plan was to just keep going, but to keep my end of the deal by keeping things in check.

Dumbass, you're the one writing the song, I thought.

So I sat and tried to write a different verse, one where I was putting a stop to Rose and I's friends with benefits arrangement, where I recognized the danger I was in and saved myself from it. I repeated the melody on the piano, and tried to let the words come.

And they just…didn't.

I stared out of my bedroom window. The way I saw it, I had two options. One was to keep going with Rose until the deadline we had already set, and just try to keep things under control. The second option was to come up with some reason to end things.

In the back of my mind, a small voice whispered that there was a third option. It was possible that Rose actually also had feelings for me, but the chances of that felt so slim that it didn't even make sense to think about it. Why the hell would Rose have feelings for *me*? I swear like an idiot and snap at people when I'm irritated and am a general nightmare. Rose was so sweet and compassionate and level-headed that sometimes I was surprised Rose was even *friends* with me. I couldn't imagine her wanting more. I didn't want to inflict that on her. Plus, Oregon Rule.

The extra dumb thing about this was that the one

person I wanted to talk things out *with* was the person I was trying to figure my shit out *about.*

"Hey Felix, we're going for burgers, you wanna come?"

I looked up to see Wendy leaning in my doorway. Fuck it, I could use a distraction. "Sure," I said.

Simon and Aaron argued good-naturedly about the best kind of French fry on the drive to the burger place, and Wendy refused to take part but egged each of them on. I also refused to take part. (Even though Aaron was right, waffle fries were the best kind of fries.)

When we were all seated in a booth and eating, Simon turned to me. "What's on your mind, Felix?"

I glared at him.

"You haven't said a word all night," he added.

"You haven't said anything for me to reply to," I said.

"Fine, how are things with Rose?"

Cool. The one thing I did not want to talk about.

"Rose is fine," I said, taking a bite of my burger.

Wendy nudged my shoulder. "He didn't ask you how Rose was, he asked you how things were going with her."

"Why is it any of your business?" I snapped. Everyone stared at me. I sighed. "Sorry."

"You can plead the fifth if you want," Aaron said. "We're not trying to pry. We're just here if you want to talk about anything."

When I looked up, his face was open and honest. Everyone else was nodding, eating their food. My chest squeezed. There was a part of me that still couldn't believe I had landed here with them, that my life had happened in just the right way to lead me here. I had a friend group and we made music together. I had people to play video games with and I would always have a ride to the airport and right now I was sitting and eating burgers with them on a Tuesday night. I spent the first part of my life being so fucking lonely all the time. What would I do if I lost these guys? If the Boy Scouts of Atlantis or Queenscout were to break up...shit, I couldn't even think about what I would do.

If I told Rose I was catching feelings, our friendship would be destroyed. I knew it would be. Because this whole thing was just supposed to be casual, and the idea of her rejecting my more serious feelings made me feel like I was literally going to die. And we couldn't actually date because of the Oregon Rule. And it felt way too shitty to just tell her that I changed my mind. Because I knew Rose—even if this whole thing was casual, she would still feel rejected, and I couldn't stand the idea of hurting her. So there was only one option.

I would, for once in my goddamn life, do something unselfish. I would do this for her. I could survive until August, giving her this gift, and then we would stop, and I could get my head on straight again, and everything would be fine. It was just a temporary crush.

"I don't want to talk about it," I said. "But I'll let you know if I change my mind."

"Definitely, man," Aaron replied. He picked up a potato wedge from his plate and held it up to the group. "I don't care what any of you people say, this is the worst type of french fry."

The argument about fries started up again, and I let it surround me, trying to hold on to the best things I had.

Ball and Chain

By Rose Devangelo

I am eighteen,
and it almost happened tonight.
A drunken man swaying
his lips towards mine,
slurring that I was beautiful.
I realized later
that his name meant "bad."
The opposite of lucky.

If I were lucky,
I would have been moving my body
in rhythm with music,
on the inside
where a boy I know
was letting songs
jump through his veins.

College is when we're supposed
to make bad decisions with strangers
and all I want is to move
with the person I know best.

CHAPTER 25

I Don't Belong Here

FRESHMAN YEAR OF HIGH SCHOOL, AGE 14

FELIX

My mom and I stared up at the two-story house in front of us.

"I had no idea your friends were rich," she said.

The fellow freshmen who had invited me to this party weren't exactly my friends, but I didn't want to tell my mom that I spent most lunchtimes alone in the library, so I didn't say anything.

"Do you have your swimsuit?" she asked.

"I'm literally wearing it," I replied.

"Did they say you need to bring your own towel? I brought a towel in case."

"I'm sure they have towels, Mom." I climbed out of the car.

"Text me when you're ready to come home," she said, leaning toward the open door. She was trying to hide her own excitement for me, and it was *agonizing*.

"Right, yes, Mom, thank you, goodbye." I watched her pull away, then took a few shaky steps toward the door.

Kendra Blasio wasn't the *most* popular girl in school, but I was star-struck anyway. In the hierarchy of middle school, she had been a B-list celebrity, and she'd kept that celebrity status now that we were in high school. We'd known each other since kindergarten.

I refused to admit to anyone that I had a crush on her. (Not that I had anyone to admit it to.) I was the weird, skinny kid with floppy hair who had headphones on half of the time. She was always fresh-faced, surrounded by friends, looking like a magazine ad. I'd liked her since seventh grade, and she usually just ignored me.

Until last week, when she and two of her friends stopped me in the courtyard after school and told me they were having a pool party on Friday to celebrate the beginning of the school year. And did I want to come?

I had been totally shocked. She had asked for my phone number so she could text me the details. After she had walked away, I had stared after her, her long blonde hair swaying gently. I could smell her shampoo lingering in the air like a spell. I wondered if I had just dreamed the whole thing.

But then a text came through later that night, with an address and a time.

Holy shit, I thought. I was going to a party. At Kendra Blasio's house.

I spent way too long freaking out over the fact that it was a pool party, which meant being shirtless, until finally I decided that Kendra Blasio probably didn't expect a fellow 14-year-old to be totally ripped.

I waited until my mom had driven around the corner, and then I knocked on the front door. Kendra pulled it open, and for a second, I couldn't think. Her long hair was wet and clinging to her bare shoulders. She was wearing a bikini top and jean shorts.

She was the most beautiful girl I had ever seen.

"Oh, Felix," she said, smiling. "Hello."

She made no motion to let me in. Two other girls appeared behind her. I recognized them, but couldn't quite remember their names. All three of them were in bathing suits, their hair wet. Their faces split into grins when they saw me.

The rest of the house was silent behind them.

"Am I…early?" I asked.

One of the girls giggled. "No, you're not early."

I stood there on the front step, not sure what to do. "Sorry, you said the party started at 7," I said.

"No, the party *ended* at 7," the other girl said. Her voice dripped with mock sympathy.

My stomach dropped. The three girls all looked at me with the same exaggerated pity. Kendra looked strangely triumphant, her arms folded in front of her chest.

"Sorry," I mumbled. "I must have made a mistake."

For one tiny second, I imagined them inviting me in anyway. I imagined us all making the most of a miscommunication, drinking sodas and swimming in the pool. We'd all laugh about it at the lunch table next week. It would be an inside joke we'd have for years.

"Whoops," Kendra said. Then she shut the door.

I heard all three of them erupt into laughter. I caught Kendra's voice saying, "I can't believe he actually came!"

I couldn't bring myself to text my mom. So I walked the three miles home, my eyes stinging the whole time.

When I got home, I ignored my mom, which made me feel even shittier, but I didn't know how to explain why I was back so early. Instead I slammed my door, collapsed onto my bed, and stared at the ceiling. Maybe I really had made a mistake about the time? I felt a tiny flutter of hope rise up in my chest. I pulled my phone out to check the text. No, it said, "Be there at 7."

I hadn't made a mistake. And neither had they. They had done it on purpose. They told me, "Be there at 7," knowing I would be.

Why the hell did I think I was actually invited to a pool party at Kendra Blasio's house? And actually, why the hell did I even like Kendra Blasio? Sure, she was pretty, but she was *mean*. Now that I really thought about it, I couldn't think of a single actual thing I liked about her. What did I think was going to happen? That I'd go to this party, and we'd spend all night talking about obscure music? That she would be impressed by my knowledge of American shipwrecks?

I was an idiot. Of course that was never going to happen. Kendra and her friends played some weird prank on me and that was it.

What was the point of it? What the hell was the point of the cruelty? I couldn't figure out what I'd ever done wrong, at any point growing up. Did I wear the wrong shoes? Was my backpack not the right height on my back? Even if those were the reasons, they were the stupidest reasons I'd ever heard of to be cruel to someone. Like, literally, it did not matter.

It had been this way for years. Kids snickering when I tried to join a game of kickball. Someone making fun of me answering a question correctly in class. Sneering at my second-hand t-shirts. It was like they had just arbitrarily picked someone to leave out and be mean to, and it happened to be me.

I was so damn tired of it. Of always being left out. Being teased. Being the weirdo creep sitting in the library all the time.

Well, then, I thought, *fuck it*. If they were gonna treat me like a freak, then was gonna *be* a freak. And I'd find my own freak friends and we'd talk about cool shit and we wouldn't be cruel to each other or to anyone else.

I started wearing black eyeliner the next day. I walked downtown to the thrift shop and used my allowance to buy as much black clothing as I could. I dyed my hair black and started letting it grow out.

And when I signed up for tech theatre the next semester, I discovered that Mrs. Tadema's classroom was full of fellow freaks, kids who wore headphones between classes like I did, and went and got Korean food for lunch and watched horror movies on the weekends. And they didn't treat me like a creep or a weirdo, because they were all creeps and weirdos, too.

During the second week of class, one of the juniors asked me what kind of music I liked, and he nodded his head when I answered. He asked me if I wanted to help him run sound, and finally, *finally*, I had found my people.

And once I had that, I didn't want to leave any of the other weird kids behind. I tried to notice when people were extra quiet, when they ate alone. Because I knew how it felt. And if no one else in this stupid nightmare of a school was going to befriend them, then I was.

My black hair and clothing became a signal. Popular kids, stay away. Freaks and weirdos, you're safe with me.

CHAPTER 26

Restless in my Soul

ROSE

I t had been two days since I'd seen Felix last and I was trying very hard to not freak out.

I stuck the moisture meter in the soil of the snake plant by my bedroom door, trying to focus. This one was good. I moved on to the string of pearls on the shelf nearby.

That last time with Felix had felt different. I knew I didn't have much experience, but it had felt more intimate, somehow. It had felt like more than having sex. It had felt like…well, like making love.

The string of pearls needed water. I lifted the can and poured some into the dish below the pot, letting the plant's roots drink what it needed.

After Felix left that day, I also realized that we hadn't really talked about it beforehand like we had the other times. There had been a kind of "container" before—a "now we are doing this" that kept everything in its proper place as a friends-with-benefits arrangement. But having sex with Felix after starting to listen to an album was the kind of night I imagined we would have together if he were really my boyfriend.

I had thought about texting him, but I wasn't sure what to say. I couldn't figure out how to articulate to him what I was feeling. I just had a vague sense of unease. Some feeling that Felix and I were connected in a new way and disconnected in the old one.

The hens-and-chicks plants in the window were fine, but the burro's tail needed water. I lifted the watering can absently.

Every now and then, in certain corners of the internet, I stumbled upon this asinine idea that when a girl has sex for the first time, she becomes especially attached to the person she does it with. As if we're all baby ducks imprinting on the first penis that touches our vaginas. And I absolutely refused to believe that was real.

But also, my soul felt all tangled up in his. I missed Felix like an ache in my center. I felt his absence more deeply than I ever had before. And I'd loved him long before we'd ever even kissed.

I felt a drip of water on my toes, and looked up to see that I'd overwatered the burro's tail. I sighed and put the watering can and soil moisture meter on the ground, then collapsed onto my bed.

I was staring up at the ceiling, trying to organize my thoughts, when Jem stopped in my doorway.

"Band practice in an hour?" she said.

I turned to her and nodded, and she studied me for a moment.

"You okay?" she asked.

I swallowed. "Just…restless. I think."

"You're literally resting right now."

"Restless in my soul," I sighed.

Jem folded her arms and leaned in my doorframe. "What does your soul need?"

"I don't know."

Jem raised her eyebrows at me. "Is that an honest answer?"

A half a dozen replies floated through my head. My soul needed belonging, it needed Felix, it needed to feel fed and safe, it needed to move through life without a hopeless ball and chain of unrequited love attached to it. I glanced around the room.

"My soul needs to tidy something."

Jem smiled, a rare soft smile. "I'll leave you to it, then."

I pulled boxes down from my closet shelves, spreading their contents on the floor. I started putting things in piles. Maybe as I sorted all of this, my thoughts and feelings could get sorted, too.

I made a pile of old ticket stubs, to be pasted into a journal. Old tax returns could be shredded, and I could recycle the old notebooks I still had from college. I tipped out a small cardboard box to find it full of mementos—stickers, postcards, a matchbook from a restaurant that still had matchbooks. In the middle of the pile sat a dull Indian-head penny.

I picked it up and smiled. Coos Bay, last year. Felix had found it while we were on a walk, and then told me about a shipwreck from the twenties. I closed my eyes and remembered the sudden way he had put his arm around me, kissed my head before continuing to walk along the beach.

If I could have gone back in time and told that Rose that she and Felix would be having sex in a year's time, she would have fainted on the spot. And then she would have woken up and demanded an explanation of how all of her dreams had come true.

I frowned. I supposed her dreams hadn't quite fully

come true. I now knew what Felix looked like without his clothes on. I knew how it felt to have Felix moving inside me. His lips against mine, the way his breathing got ragged when he was getting close.

But I didn't know what it felt like to have him kiss me goodbye after a show. I didn't know what it felt like to hold hands while we walked to get ice cream with our friends after a gig. To move my body against his while we listened to a band play in a dark venue.

I didn't know what it felt like for him to be my actual boyfriend. To truly be with me, claim me as his own, let me claim him back.

The thought sent a stab of pain through my ribs.

Was it worth it?

I could almost hear Rose of one year ago asking me the question. I didn't know how to answer her. I wouldn't trade the last few weeks with Felix for the world. And yet...

Whenever Felix *wasn't* with me, I felt so alone. More than I had when we were just friends. He'd left my room so suddenly two days ago. He didn't even look at me as he put his clothes on. My bed had felt so cold without him in it.

If I was being really truly honest with myself, sex with Felix wasn't enough. I wanted love with Felix.

I glanced at the calendar. We still had two full months before our August 12 deadline. I thought about us having sex in my room, looking into each others' eyes while we moved together, and then not touching outside of my room. He felt so connected in those moments in my bed. Like we were truly seeing each other for the first time in our nine years of being friends. And then later, he acted like everything was the same as always, when I knew it wasn't. I couldn't get it to make sense.

You're tearing yourself apart for him, I thought. *Still.* I closed my eyes. If he hadn't asked me to be his girlfriend after all these years, then he probably never would.

I realized with a sinking feeling that some part of me still secretly hoped that us sleeping together would change his mind somehow, make him realize how much we belonged together. But I imagined explaining this situation to a friend, and I could hear how delusional it sounded.

What I desperately wanted was…well, all of it. I wanted the Felix who made my naked body feel alive and connected and I wanted the Felix who went on walks on the beach with me. But something had shifted in the last few days, and the distance between those two Felixes was growing. And I couldn't imagine my life without at least some version of Felix in it.

I knew I couldn't keep the Felix who touched my body. So I'd have to choose the one who was just my friend.

My stomach lurched. Did knowing this change anything? I tried to picture keeping this thing going with him, but I couldn't imagine another moment when his lips touched mine without it wrecking me. I just couldn't keep giving myself something that couldn't last.

Which meant, if I was truly caring for my own heart, I had to break it off. Now.

A sob wrenched my throat, and I covered my mouth to stifle it. I held back my tears as I slowly sorted through the rest of the things I'd pulled from my closet. I tried to talk myself into and then out of just one more time with Felix. There were still things I wanted to try, and I couldn't imagine doing them with anyone else.

But there was a calm, solid part of me, deep down, that knew that it was time for me to show my own heart the care it so desperately longed for. I knew that continuing this thing with Felix would unravel me deeply. I knew that if I had answered Jem's question with complete honesty, I would have told her that the thing my soul needed was to be honored in all of its tenderness.

By the time I closed my eyes that night, I had a draft of what I would say to him written.

CHAPTER 27

A Dream That I Could Speak To

SENIOR YEAR OF HIGH SCHOOL, AGE 17

ROSE

I had to ask him. Before he got on the bus to go home. Prom was next week, and I'd spent a whole month trying to work up the courage to ask Felix to be my date. It didn't even have to be romantic. We could just go as friends. I couldn't think of anyone else in the world I'd rather go with, and senior prom was supposed to be one of those milestone high school experiences. I already had a dress. I just needed a date.

The bell rang, and I watched him stand up on the other side of the drama room. *You have to do it*, I thought.

"Felix!" I called out.

He turned as I crossed the room to stand in front of him. "Hey."

"Hi." And then I just sort of stood there for a moment. Felix raised his eyebrows at me. "Sorry. Um…I was just wondering. Um."

"Yeah?"

I took in his features—the sharp green eyes, lined in black, the dark hair. The words rushed out of me. "I-was-wondering-if-you-wanted-to-go-to-prom-with-me?"

"Oh. Shit," Felix said. "I'm already going with Xalia. Did she not tell you?"

The room tilted, and for a moment I couldn't quite breathe. "Xalia?" I repeated.

"Yeah," Felix shrugged. "Just as friends. She wanted to go with Rachel, but Rachel's out of town that weekend."

"No, that's…that's totally fine," I said, trying to keep my voice casual. I could feel the tremble in my lungs right below the surface. "I didn't know, but…that's fine."

"You could come with us, too, if you want," Felix offered. "Throuple it up."

His words drew a genuine smile from me, even if it was a small one. "That's all right," I said. "Lanie was also looking for a date, so I might go with her. Also just as friends."

"Cool," Felix said. "See you Monday?"

"See you Monday," I replied.

I managed to make it two blocks before the tears started. It wasn't just that I wouldn't be able to go to my senior prom with Felix. It was the casual and friendly way he'd declined. Like he wasn't sad about it at all.

I KNEW that the day before prom was not a good time to make drastic hair decisions, but my bruised heart didn't listen. I needed a change and I needed it badly. So as soon as school got out on Friday afternoon, I walked into a salon and asked them to give me a pixie cut.

And even though it felt impulsive, when I looked into the mirror, I was glad I'd made the choice. My hair fell in soft short waves around my face, making me look whimsical and cute. In my long, flowing, red prom dress, I would look like a woodland fairy.

I had decided that going to prom with a friend was better than not going to prom at all. I knew I would be miserable if I just stayed home, staring at the dress I'd bought. So I'd asked Lanie if she wanted to be my platonic date, and she was meeting me at the venue in half an hour. At least I'd be able to hang out with Felix if I went to prom. And even though I felt foolish about it, I longed to have at least one dance with him, and that couldn't happen unless I was there.

My mom insisted on taking half a dozen pictures of me in my dress before I left, and then she handed me her car keys and told me to be safe.

Our senior class had raised enough money to hold prom in a local greenhouse/nursery, and when I stepped into the room, it took my breath away for a moment. String lights glowed softly among the branches of what seemed like hundreds of small trees, and flowers surrounded every pathway. The air was warm and humid, fogging up the tall glass windows and ceiling. Deeper into the room, there was a large dance floor, and twenty or thirty of my classmates were already jumping around to the music.

"Rose!" a voice called.

I turned to see Felix a few feet away. He looked incredible. He was wearing a black shirt with tuxedo ruffles down the front, tuxedo pants, and a leather jacket. His black boots had silver spikes on them, and I could see a pair of suspenders peeking out from beneath his jacket. His dark hair was falling into his eyes in the perfect way it always did.

Felix came and stood a few feet away from me, taking me in. "I like your hair," he said, speaking over the music. "You're like a softer version of Alice Cullen."

I smiled at him, then reached up to touch my short waves. "Thanks," I replied. His compliment was making it hard to find my voice, but I finally managed to add, "Your outfit is amazing. Also very vampiric. In like, a punk rock way. You're a punk rock vampire."

He smiled back at me and my breath caught. His smile always knocked me flat, every time. "Did you bring Lanie?" he asked.

"I'm meeting her here," I replied. I paused, and then added, "Is Xalia here?"

Felix nodded, then turned to look deeper into the greenhouse. "She's grabbing something to drink." He turned back to me, and we stood there in the dim light for a moment, looking at each other.

My thoughts were interrupted by someone else calling out my name. I turned to see Lanie walking toward me.

"Hi!" I said, hugging her. When I pulled away, Xalia had showed up, and all four of us made our way to the dance floor.

You wouldn't think of Felix as the kind of guy who loved dancing. But Felix loved music, and dancing was one of his ways of expressing it. The four of us spent hours dancing together, occasionally going our separate ways to say hi to others we knew, using the slow songs to rest or sip from plastic cups of watery fruit punch.

As the clock ticked toward 11 pm, I kept glancing over at Felix. I just wanted one dance with just him. Just one. But every time a slow song came on, he left the floor. And the more I thought about asking him to dance, the sillier I felt. I don't know if I could pinpoint exactly why. Maybe the *amount* I wanted it was what made me feel silly. It was just a dance. But I wanted it.

Finally, the DJ spoke into the mic.

"All right. Here's the last dance of the night. Find that special someone and pull them into your arms. Like the woman said, 'at last.'"

The sweetly aching words of Etta James' famous ballad filled the air. This was it. My last chance to dance with Felix. It was now or never. My hands clutched at my long dress as I scanned the room.

There. On the other side of the floor, leaning against a tree, looking like a dark fairy tale prince. Felix had taken his leather jacket off, but he still looked mysterious and beautiful. He was the best friend I'd ever had, and the only person whose arms I wanted around me at the end of tonight.

All I had to do was cross the floor and ask him. That was all I had to do.

But my feet were frozen in place. My blood thudded through my veins so loudly it was almost drowning out the music. I closed my eyes and took a deep breath.

When I opened them, Felix was leading Xalia out onto the dance floor, a friendly smile on his face.

My heart cracked. I sank onto a low stone bench.

Felix's arms snaked around Xalia's waist, and she rested her hands on his shoulders. I watched as they swayed in a slow circle, chatting occasionally. I used to wonder if Felix had feelings for Xalia, but from everything I knew, they were just friends. Just friends dancing together at prom.

Every single part of me ached.

Would he ever love me the way I loved him? Would he ever see my face and think, "Yes, her. That's who I want"?

Watching Felix on the dance floor, with Etta James singing about her lonely days being over, it was hard to imagine him seeing me as anything more than a friend.

So I sat, longing, watching the boy I loved most in the world dance with someone else.

CHAPTER 28

Friends Quest

FELIX

When I opened the front door, Rose was standing with her arms wrapped around herself, looking uncertain.

"Hey," I frowned. Then I took in her posture. "Are you okay?"

"Wanna go for a walk?" she asked.

My frown deepened. When Rose texted to ask if she could come over, my heart had leapt happily. And then it had squeezed with anxiety. Because my heart was absolutely not supposed to be leaping happily about Rose coming over. Unless it was in a platonic way. *You're being unselfish*, I reminded myself. *You're putting aside your own feelings so that Rose can have this gift.* It was the least I could do for her, after all the things she'd done for me.

Bonus: if I could set aside my own feelings, then maybe they wouldn't get hurt.

I had spent an hour cleaning my room, but Rose had just suggested a walk, and going on a walk meant we weren't going to spend time in my room. I grabbed my keys and stepped outside.

"Sure," I said.

We made our way to Alameda Beach in silence. For once in my life, I couldn't figure out what the hell she was thinking. When we got to the sand, Rose sat down and patted the ground beside her. We both sat and watched the water of the Bay for a few minutes.

"Thanks for coming here with me today," she said. Her words were oddly formal.

I raised my eyebrows. "I feel like I'm about to get fired," I replied.

Rose gave me a small, closed-lip smile.

Shit fuck. What was happening?

"I've been thinking," Rose said.

Everything inside of me clenched, bracing for impact. "Yeah?" I asked.

She turned and looked at me, and I ached with affection for her. Her short hair was messier than usual in the breeze, and her small soft mouth looked so kissable. But her brown eyes were troubled. She looked back out at the water again.

"I can't tell you how grateful I am that you were my first," she said quietly. "My first kiss, and my first…everything else. Really. I couldn't imagine it with anyone else."

I swallowed. "You're welcome," I said. If I said anything else, I was gonna give myself away.

"I know when we started this, we gave it a deadline," Rose said. "But I think I got what I needed. I think—"

She cut herself off and it was like her words were a rope that I was clinging to, hanging off a cliff. Whatever she said next would either pull me up or drop me into the chasm.

"I think I'd like to stop now," she finished.

It was the chasm. I felt myself drop, panic and sorrow waiting to envelop me when I hit the bottom.

Rose turned to me, looking tortured. "I care about you so much," she said. "I didn't want this thing we were doing to get in the way of our friendship. Felix, I can't imagine not having you as my friend."

I looked away, trying to gather my thoughts. A very significant part of me wanted to grab her shoulders and say, "No! We can keep doing this and stay friends the way we always have been!" But I knew it wasn't true. It hadn't been true since the night we listened to the album together. Maybe longer. If we kept kissing, if we kept sleeping together, just friendship alone would become less and less satisfying to me. I had seen what I wanted, but pursuing it meant destroying the thing I already had.

I cleared my throat. "So, no more Sex Quest?" I asked.

Rose smiled sadly. "No more Sex Quest. But friends?"

I nodded. "Friends Quest."

We sat in silence for a few more moments before I started truly spiraling.

What had brought this on for her? Did she suspect that I was starting to feel something more for her? Is that why she was pulling the plug on this? To spare my feelings?

Or what if I had done something? What if I had made her uncomfortable, or crossed a line or something? I tried to think back over all the times we'd hooked up, trying to see if there was something I'd missed, some sign that she wasn't into it.

"Hey, Felix?" Rose asked.

I turned to her, my thoughts still racing. "Yeah?"

Her eyes searched my face. "Are you crashing out over this?"

Fuck, she knew me so well. I thought about lying, but after being friends for a decade, I knew she wouldn't believe me. "A little," I replied. I took a deep breath, then decided to ask at least one of the questions that was swirling around in my brain. "Did I ever...?" I paused while I tried to figure out how to phrase it. "Did I ever cross a line with you? Like, physically? Did I ever do anything that you were uncomfortable with?"

Rose's eyes widened and she grabbed my arm. Even now, the touch made my skin tingle. "No!" she said. "Felix! God, no. That's not what this is about. At all." I nodded, but my relief didn't feel complete. Rose softened. "Everything that we did was completely consensual," she said quietly. "I would do it all again."

"I would, too." It slipped out before I could stop it. I didn't mean to say it.

Rose's eyes snapped to mine, searching. My words hovered in the air between us, taking on more weight the longer we looked at each other. Finally, Rose turned away.

"You never made me uncomfortable," she said, finally.

"Good," I replied.

At least there was that.

Rose pulled her knees up and rested her chin on them. "What will we tell the others?" she asked.

Jesus, I hadn't even thought of that. "We can just tell them that the uh, arrangement is done and that we're back to being just friends."

Rose nodded. And then we sat, side by side, for another twenty minutes, watching the waves, not talking.

Finally, Rose stood, then held a hand out to help me up. I took it and then stood in front of her.

"Do you still wanna hang out?" I asked. "Tonight, I mean?"

Rose studied me. "I think...I think I'm going to go home? If that's okay?"

"Totally fine," I said. We walked a few blocks together

before parting ways to go to our separate houses. As soon as I was on my own, the whole afternoon came plummeting down onto me. I actually had to lean over for a second to try and catch my breath.

What I should have been feeling in this moment was relief. I had been ready to embark on a difficult two-month exercise in selflessness, where I hid a crush on my best friend so that she could experience sex. That problem was now solved. And I had been afraid of Rose and I's friendship being sabotaged—that was solved, too. She clearly didn't want our friendship to be ruined, and I didn't either, so that meant we were on the same page.

So then why did I feel so miserable?

When I got back home, the other guys looked up from where they were playing video games. Wendy did a double take and then paused the game.

"Hey, are you okay?" he asked.

I shrugged. "I think I just got dumped," I said. I had meant for it to sound like a joke, but it did not land.

My bandmates exchanged glances. "Did you end things with Rose?" Simon asked.

"We decided it's better for us to just be friends," I replied. Really *she* decided that, but I was trying to soften the blow for both them and myself. I was fighting like hell to keep my voice steady. "She got what she needed out of the arrangement, so it's done."

Wendy, Simon, and Aaron all sat on the couch and looked at me, concern in their eyes. A wave of irritation washed over me. "Guys, I'm *fine*," I said. "We weren't actually *dating*. I was making a *joke*."

"Wanna play Battlefront?" Wendy said.

"No."

"Okay," Aaron said. "You just look sad."

"I'm a dumb emo kid, I always look sad," I said. Then

I walked down the hallway to my room, shut the door, and started digging through my records. When I had found something sufficiently loud, I collapsed onto my bed.

I hated the way Simon had phrased that. *"Did you end things with Rose?"* It made it sound like the thing with Rose had been real. But it hadn't been. Like every other time in my life.

It hadn't been real with Kendra freshman year of high school, and it hadn't been real with Eva in college, and of course it hadn't been real with Rose. I was always the one left standing with my heart in my hands.

Thank god it hadn't gotten any further. At least I still had Rose's friendship. Even if, right now, I couldn't imagine seeing her and *not* kissing her.

Fuck. I hated this. I turned off the music and went back into the living room.

"I changed my mind, gimme a controller," I said.

But no matter how many stormtroopers I killed, I couldn't get the ache in my center to completely go away.

CHAPTER 29

What Your Heart Needs

FELIX

Simon was singing his ass off and I was playing like absolute shit. And I seriously had no excuse. The monitor mix was fine and the crowd was only half paying attention. I was just stuck in my head and couldn't play worth a damn.

I messed up the intro to "Long Skirt, Short Jacket" but the guys covered it okay. But when I did the same thing on "Toil and Trouble," Simon frowned at me from his spot at the front. I shook my head at him and kept playing.

I knew I'd been quieter than usual during sound check, but I just didn't want to explain that even days later, I still felt like Rose had broken up with me, and I couldn't stop thinking about it. My brain kept following the same loop over and over and over again.

Had I done something wrong? No, Rose said I didn't. Did she suspect that I had started feeling more than friendship for her, and was trying to spare my feelings? It was possible, but I had no idea. Should I tell her? That I caught feelings? No, absolutely not, because if she wanted to be with me, she would have said something by now. Plus, that would ruin the best friendship I had ever known. Right? Did she really break it off just because she was done? What if I had done something wrong?

Ad infinitum.

The really dumb thing was that we said in the beginning that the music came first—that what we were doing shouldn't get in the way of playing good shows. Rose even wrote it down. But what had happened between Rose and I was making me play like a middle school idiot, and I was pretty sure I'd be playing better if I knew I could hold that girl in my arms after this set. If I knew her voice and her eyes and her kisses were waiting for me.

For one tiny second, I let myself daydream. I let myself imagine that Rose was there in the back of the venue, watching us play. After we finished our set, I'd wrap my arms around her and kiss the top of her head, and then we'd make out in the parking lot, and then back home in my bed, I'd move my mouth and hands over her until she was making those hungry sighing noises and then—

Shit fuck, I messed up another chord change. Goddammit.

It was roughly 200 degrees on the tiny stage, and the lights weren't making it any better. I hated playing this venue. They always wanted long sets and they paid like shit. But we had room in our schedule and the other guys convinced me that we might as well play it. Shit pay was better than no pay.

What I really wanted to do was sleep for like, two weeks. Or maybe be put into a coma, the way they do with burn victims, so that they don't have to suffer while they heal. I wanted a metaphorical breakup coma.

Music usually set my mind at ease, but this was one of the rare times when it wasn't working.

We finished out the song we were playing and Simon said, "We're gonna take a quick break! We'll be back in a few minutes with some more tunes!"

When we got backstage, Simon pulled me aside. "Hey, are you good, dude?"

I really *really* didn't feel like spilling my guts about Rose right now. "Fine," I said, shaking my head. "I didn't get a lot of sleep last night."

His eyes searched mine, concern etched into his face. Then, completely unexpectedly, he pulled me into a hug.

I was so surprised at first that I sort of froze. My forehead was kind of smashed against Simon's shoulder, but his arms were strong and…shit, I couldn't remember the last time someone hugged me like this. I felt like a little kid, but I wrapped my arms around him in return. Because apparently, I really fucking needed a hug right now.

I felt another set of arms come around me from behind, and I turned my face slightly to see Wendy holding me, too. Then Aaron's arms came around all of us. I huffed out a small laugh, but I didn't let go.

When I was young, I couldn't imagine friendship looking like this. Especially between men. I didn't have any examples of it growing up, and I'm not exactly the physical affection type. But right now, no one was kidding around or saying "no homo" or trying to prove anything. These guys saw that I needed a hug and they hugged me. I didn't have to say anything, but I knew they would listen if I did.

After a few minutes of just standing like that backstage, we all split apart. "Should we start the next set with 'Weird Science'?" Simon asked.

"Damn, we haven't played that in a minute," Aaron replied. "I say yes."

"I second the motion," Wendy said.

When everyone turned to me, I nodded.

WHEN WE STRODE BACK out under the lights, I was determined to play well for the second set. No more fuck-ups. I stepped behind the keyboard and looked up at Simon, waiting for him to count us off.

"We're the Boy Scouts of Atlantis, and we're back with some more songs for you all. We'd like to start out with— oh, hey!" Simon interrupted himself, and I could hear his grin. "My super hot girlfriend is here, everybody!"

My heart exploded in my chest. If Marlowe was here, did that mean…?

I shaded my eyes and looked out into the crowd. And there she was, standing a little off to the side. Rose. My sweet Rose, with her short messy hair and her warm brown eyes. So pretty. When our eyes met, she gave me a small smile. I swear to god she was actually glowing.

Simon was climbing down from the stage, after saying something into the mic about how he "needed some sugar," which made me want to throw up but also made me insanely envious because I wanted to say the same thing about Rose. I watched as Simon and Marlowe made out in front of the stage before he climbed back up to his spot.

I couldn't look away from Rose, even though looking at her made my chest ache so much I didn't know how I could stand it. Her hands were stuck in the pockets of these striped overall shorts, and I could see how she'd swept up some of her short hair into some kind of clip on one side. How the fuck did I get onto this timeline? The one where I had a crush on my best friend and knew what she looked like naked but we *weren't* together? This was dumb as shit. God, I couldn't wait for this crush to fade.

When Simon counted us off, I finally managed to tear my gaze away from Rose and focus on my keyboard.

No fuckups, I thought. *Just play.*

So I did. We played for twenty more minutes, and then our set was done, and then we were all wrapping cables and packing up gear.

"Hi," a voice said near my elbow. I froze, but didn't look up I didn't need to. I'd recognize Rose's voice anywhere in the world.

"What are you doing here?" I asked. Shit, I hadn't meant it to come out like that. Why was I such an asshole all the time?

When I looked up, Rose was frowning, which made me feel like complete garbage. "Sorry," I mumbled. "I just didn't know you'd be here."

"Marlowe convinced us all to come," Rose said. She was quiet for a long time. "Felix?" she finally said.

"Yeah?"

"That…that hurt my feelings. What you said just now." Rose's voice shook a little, and her eyes were uncertain.

I didn't think. I just dropped the cables I was holding and pulled her into my arms. Goddamn *fuck* it felt good to hold her. "I'm really sorry," I whispered into her hair. "I was being a dick. You coming to the show took me by surprise but I didn't have to be a dick about it."

"That's…thanks," Rose replied, her voice slightly muffled against my chest. "I'm trying this thing where I stick up for myself," she said. "Or I…I try to give myself what my heart needs."

My arms wrapped more tightly around her. "I hope you always get what your heart needs," I whispered. And I meant it. I held her until she finally stepped back. When she did, I saw her brush a tear away.

"Shit, I'm sorry!" I said. Again. I could not get this right.

But Rose shook her head and smiled. "It's not you," she said. "I'm just…that meant a lot to me. Thank you."

She reached out and squeezed my hand, and it took everything in me to not yank her back into my arms. God, this sucked.

But the entire reason I had started the thing with Rose in the first place was because I was trying to be selfless, to think of someone outside of myself for once in my life. And that's what I needed to do now, too.

"No problem," I said, then went back to wrapping cables.

CHAPTER 30

It's a Real Plan If We Use a White Board

ROSE

I t had been six days since we went to the Boy Scouts' show, and I'd been torturing myself about it ever since. My thoughts cycled through regret to being proud of myself to remembering the way Felix had hugged me and then despairing that it was all over. I picked up extra shifts at work, and when I was home, I either played bass or stared at the ceiling from my bed.

I was completely miserable.

After wallowing for an hour or two this afternoon, I decided I needed to do *something*, so I took six or seven succulents out to the driveway to repot them. They didn't really need it, but *I* needed it. At the last minute, I grabbed two more plants from the living room to repot them, too, balancing them carefully as I stepped outside.

Crash.

I locked down to see the pothos plant I'd been carrying in a pile of dirt on the driveway, the pot in pieces.

I burst into tears.

It was a completely unreasonable response to what had just happened. The plant was fine, and I was repotting it anyway, and I had another pot ready that wasn't broken. But I sat down in the middle of the driveway, leaned my head on my knees, and sobbed.

Which was how Jem, Ducky, and Marlowe found me when they pulled up ten minutes later.

"Rosie!" Ducky cried. I looked up and tried to swipe my tears away, but only succeeded in getting potting soil all over my face. Jem dropped down beside me and wrapped her arms around me, and then Ducky and Marlowe sat down on my other side. And then these precious friends of mine just let me cry.

When my tears had slowed, Jem spoke quietly. "Felix?" she asked.

I nodded.

"What happened?" Marlowe asked.

"We…broke up," I choked out. "Or, we stopped the friends with benefits thing. We're still friends. But not kissing anymore or anything."

Ducky nodded. "Did you end it or did he?"

"I did."

"Why?" Jem asked. I didn't answer. I didn't know how to.

"Hey Rose?" Marlowe said.

"Yeah?"

"You don't have to answer this if you don't want to," Marlowe continued. "Truly. But did you start having feelings for Felix? More than friend feelings?"

My eyes stung with a fresh wave of tears, and I took a shaky breath. I needed to say it. To be completely honest about it, for once in my life.

"I've been in love with him since we were sixteen," I whispered. I had never, in all of these years, ever said it out loud. I'd written it and thought it and felt it, but the words themselves had been left unspoken. Until now, sitting in the middle of the driveway with my bandmates.

The air hummed with my revelation, but I felt lighter than I had a few seconds ago. Like saying it out loud had released something I didn't know was weighing me down.

"I thought so," Jem said.

I looked over at her. "Was I that obvious?"

Jem shook her head. "No. I've just had my suspicions. I think you'd have to be looking really hard to notice."

"But you love him?" Marlowe asked. "You have for a long time?"

I nodded. Everyone around me was quiet for a moment.

"I think he deserves to know that," Jem finally said.

My stomach dropped, and I looked over at her. "I can't tell him," I whispered. "He'll feel deceived. Like I lied to him all this time. And it's even worse because we kissed and…did other stuff."

It felt so inaccurate to distill the things I'd done with Felix into "other stuff," but I couldn't bring myself to say anything different.

"Rose," Jem said. "You're just gonna keep torturing yourself if you don't tell him."

But I shook my head. "If I tell him, and he doesn't feel the same way, then our friendship is ruined, and so is Queenscout, and I can't do that to him. I can't do that to any of you."

Jem adjusted so that she was sitting cross-legged directly across from me. "We survived Marlowe and Simon and we can survive whatever happens or doesn't happen with you and Felix. And your friendship doesn't have to be ruined. And he might feel the same way."

"It's hard for me to believe the last part," I said, feeling small. "If he felt the same way, why hasn't he said or done anything?"

"Why haven't *you?*" Marlowe asked.

Touché.

Ducky nudged my shoulder. "How many times have you *not* gotten something you wanted just because you didn't speak up?"

I closed my eyes. The tender melody of Etta James' "At Last" echoed through my mind. The longing that I felt watching Felix dance with someone else that night was still an ache in my center.

"There have been a lot of times. I think."

The four of us sat in my driveway in silence. Ducky, Jem, and Marlowe all just sat quietly with me, all of us thinking. After a few long minutes, Ducky looked over at me.

"Since you were *sixteen?*" she asked.

When I nodded, she replied, "Damn."

"Is it…unhealthy?" I asked uncertainly. "To love one person for that long?"

"No," Jem said, almost violently. "What's unhealthy is you carrying it around like a state secret and tearing yourself to pieces over it." She watched me closely. "Rose," she said. "Loving someone will never be a problem. It's the sacrificing yourself to it part that isn't sustainable."

She stood up, then offered a hand down to me. "Come on," she said.

A wave of panic rushed over me, and I blinked up at her. "Where are we going?" I asked.

"We're making a plan," she said.

I looked over at Ducky and Marlowe, and both of

them were smiling warmly at me. Maybe I could do it. If I had a plan. If I had these three smart, caring, wonderful women in my corner.

I took Jem's hand and let her pull me up. I was getting ready to walk back into the house when she yanked me into a tight hug, crushing my lungs. I felt a rush of love for her and her intense care, even if she didn't show it in the usual ways.

Maybe that was something I appreciated in a lot of people.

After a few moments, though, it was getting hard to breathe, so I tapped Jem's back and gasped, "I'm running out of air."

Marlowe pulled us apart, smiling. "Jem's not used to being affectionate."

"Yeah, it comes out as violence," Ducky nodded.

But I squeezed Jem's hand in thanks, then glanced down at the driveway. "What about the broken pot?" I asked.

"Leave it," Jem said.

"No!" Ducky shouted.

We all turned to her.

"We should clean it up together!" Ducky said. "It's symbolic! It's healing!"

Jem was frowning skeptically, but Marlowe turned to me with another one of her tender smiles, then bent down to pick up one of the broken shards of the pot. Her suggestion was a little on the nose, but I adored her for making it.

I grabbed an empty pot and filled it partway with soil, then arranged the pothos plant inside of it, packing more soil around it. Jem went and grabbed a broom from the house, and Marlowe started carrying the other succulents back inside.

Finally, all four of us gathered in the living room.

"Okay," Jem said. "Let's—"

"Wait!" Ducky cried. She walked into the kitchen and then brought back the giant four foot by four foot white board we usually used for reminders and scheduling. She grinned at us. "It's a real plan if we use a white-board."

Jem sighed and rolled her eyes. "Thank you, Ducky."

"Let me know if you need me to make a flow chart," she said, uncapping a marker.

"Actually," I said. "That might be a good idea."

Ducky looked at me and then held out the marker. I stood and walked to the white board and then drew two bubbles. In one, I wrote "Tell Felix" and in the other, I wrote "Don't tell Felix."

"Perfect," Ducky said. She ran to the kitchen and grabbed another marker, then drew a line from the "Tell Felix" bubble. Under it, she wrote, "He feels the same way." When she saw the doubtful look on my face, she said, "A good flow chart should list every single possibility!"

I still had a hard time believing her, but I nodded. And then we started building the flow chart. My heart was still humming with fear and heartbreak, but I felt like I could breathe normally if I had these women by my side, helping me figure it out.

After we'd talked things through, we all sat back and looked at what we'd written.

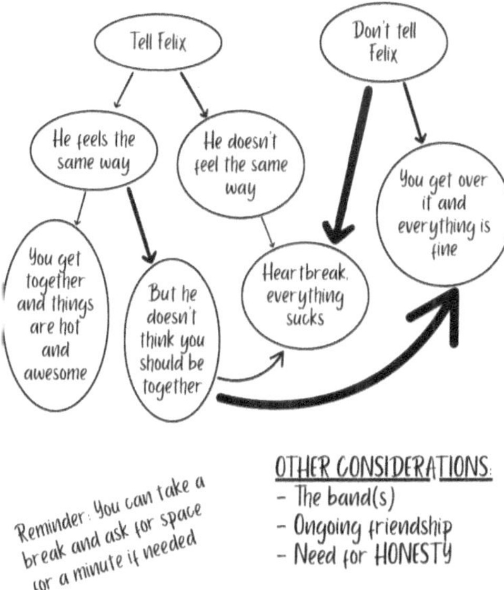

"So we have three possible outcomes," Jem said. "One is that you get together and things are hot and awesome. Two is heartbreak and everything sucking, and three is you get over it and everything's fine." She turned to me. "Knowing all of this, and taking into consideration the other factors, how would you like to move forward?"

I smiled. Jem's militaristic nature was truly coming in handy right now. I studied the board.

"I'm still really afraid of the heartbreak and everything sucking outcome," I said.

"Reasonable," Ducky replied. "I want to point out that you might also get over it and everything could be fine."

I took a deep breath and nodded. "But if there's even the smallest chance of us being together…"

I looked at the faces of my three friends. All of them nodded at me, and then gathered around and pulled me into a hug.

CHAPTER 31

Are You Having a Stroke or a Revelation?

FELIX

Aaron looked down at his phone screen and let out a despairing groan from his spot on the couch. All four of us were in the living room, scrolling on our individual phones but still in each other's company.

Which, honestly, was what I needed. I didn't want to *talk* to anyone, but being alone also felt shit-damn awful. Being alone *around* my bandmates was working.

"Did that girl ghost you again?" Simon asked.

"Yes!" Aaron exclaimed. "If you get busy, I understand, but don't leave a guy hanging!"

Wendy gave him a sympathetic smile. "Sorry, dude."

"Maybe I just don't know how to date," Aaron said, staring up at the ceiling. "I just need…what is it called when you marry someone just for convenience?"

"A marriage of convenience?" Simon asked, hiding a smile.

"Yeah, that," Aaron replied. "Or an arranged marriage or something. I don't think I even know what love is.

Honestly. If I went on a date with this girl, how would I even know what love felt like? There's gotta be some way to measure it."

"Aaron, you have a crush on half of the people you meet!" Wendy accused.

"Yeah, but that's different," Aaron replied. "A crush is the fun, drawn-to-them slash they're-attractive feeling. What's the difference between that and *love*?"

Simon looked thoughtful. "When my mom had cancer," he said, "my dad told me that even when she was bald and throwing up and pale, she was still beautiful to him. And I've used that as a measure of love ever since. Like, if Marlowe was bald and throwing up and pale, I'd still feel the same about her."

I stared at the carpet. Had there ever been anyone I felt that way about?

Well, Rose. Obviously.

Wait. My stomach lurched.

"And I guess sometimes you just know," Simon added. "My grandparents danced all night together before they knew each other's names. At the end of the night, they were dragged apart by their friends and my grandpa yelled 'Do you want to go on a date?' and my grandma yelled back 'When?' And then my grandpa gave her the name of a train station downtown and a time, and when my grandma showed up, they told each other their names, and then they got married two months later."

"Two months?" Wendy asked.

Simon shrugged. "Their 60th wedding anniversary is coming up. When you know, you know."

"Man, things were so romantic back when we had train stations," Aaron said. "Maybe I would understand romantic love better if I spent more time at train stations."

"In my opinion, romantic love is just friendship plus sex," Wendy said.

Aaron leaned back and put his hands behind his head. "Maybe I think that's actually what a crush is. Friendship plus sex. And maybe love is *that* but more intense."

"This is going to sound trite," Wendy added, "but I once heard that love is seeing right through someone and still enjoying the view."

"We love a trite saying," Simon smiled. "Love is a crush intensified and also seeing someone's flaws and wanting to walk by their side anyway."

Wait. *Wait.*

WAIT!

"Whoa. Felix?" Simon asked.

I looked over at him with wide eyes and realized that I had jumped to my feet. "Huh?"

"Are you okay?"

My whole body was shaking slightly, and I felt like I couldn't quite breathe. Actually, I was almost light-headed. I sank back down into my chair then leaned my head down between my knees.

Because all of a sudden, I was consumed with a single thought.

Was I in love with Rose? Holy goddamn shit, *was I in love with Rose Devangelo?*

What I felt for her was at least deep friendship. It always had been. But in the last month or so, that affection had deepened. And kissing her and having sex with her had felt so right—like it was the perfect expression of how I felt. I had come to know Rose in a deeper way, and I still wanted her by my side. And hell, if someone had dragged her away from me at the end of a long night of hanging out, I'd ask to see her again too, even if I didn't know her name.

There were always things I had loved about Rose. I loved Rose's compassion. I loved the way she quietly took care of everyone and everything around her. I loved her deep love of music, and the way she played bass like she was living inside of the song. I loved how she found something to love in everyone and everything around her—the way she nurtured without even trying.

And I loved the way she kissed. I loved the way her hands felt on my body. Even now, my arms ached to hold her, to touch her skin, to feel her soft warmth.

Aaron's face appeared in my field of vision. "Are you good, man?"

I blinked up at him. "I'm…"

"You're…?" Aaron asked.

"I'm an idiot," I finished. I lifted my head and then slumped backwards into the chair, clutching at my hair. "Oh my shitting god, I'm a fucking idiot."

All three of my fellow bandmates stared at me.

"Rose," I managed, my voice sounding strangled.

"What do you mean?" Wendy asked.

I was having a hard time putting words together. "I might be…I didn't realize that…shit, maybe it went too far, but I couldn't help…"

Simon grabbed both of my shoulders. "Felix," he said. "Are you having a stroke or a revelation?"

"Revelation," I replied.

"And is it about Rose?" he asked next.

I nodded. When everyone looked at me expectantly, I finally managed to say, "I might be in love with Rose." Saying it out loud was making me feel kind of light-headed again, so I gripped Simon's arms to steady myself.

"Jesus, dude," Wendy said. "You look like you're about to pass out. Come here."

I let Simon and Wendy guide me to the floor, where I laid down and stared at the ceiling.

"So you finally realized that you're in love with Rose?" Simon asked. His voice came from near my head, and I saw that he had laid down nearby. When I lifted my head for a second, I saw that all three of my bandmates were laying on the floor.

I laid my head back down. "I think so," I said.

"I hate to say this," Simon said, "but no shit, dude."

I turned to glare at him, but he just shrugged.

"He's right," Aaron added. "I'm pretty sure you've been in love with her for a while."

The white patterned ceiling swam above me.

Wendy was quiet for a moment before he asked, "Did you feel this way before or after you started doing the kissing, hooking up thing?"

I thought back over the last month or so, and then the past decade. I'd loved Rose since high school. I knew that. I'd always known that. But I wasn't sure if I was in love with her until…maybe it was the night we listened to the Stonewallflower album?

"Love before, in love after," I answered.

"So when are you gonna tell her?" Aaron asked.

I was still so busy trying to process my realization that I hadn't even thought about what to do about it. Aaron's question made my stomach clench with dread. "I can't," I said quietly.

Aaron sat up and looked down at me. "Why not?"

"Because," I said, looking up at him. "She wanted a casual, no-strings-attached, friends-with-benefits thing. She specifically wanted to do stuff with no stakes. If I tell her I caught feelings, she'll never trust me again."

"Who says?" Wendy asked.

"I mean…" I started to protest but trailed off when I

realized that Wendy might have a good point. It was true that Rose might not trust me again, but maybe she would. She was like, the most understanding person I knew.

But even if she understood, it would just make her feel bad, and then everything would be awkward at best and miserable at worst. And what was the point of telling her if she didn't want to be with me?

"If I tell her and things get weird, everything is ruined," I said.

"So you just choosing to carry a torch for your best friend is *not* going to ruin things?" Simon asked.

"Shit," I replied.

Aaron laid back down and the four of us looked up at the ceiling. "Can you picture yourself doing shows with Rose, going to her house, spending time with her, and her not knowing your feelings?"

The idea slammed into me like a ton of bricks. "I don't want to," I said.

"So tell her!" Aaron replied.

"But you don't get it," I said, sitting up. "What if she doesn't feel the same way? I'm gonna tell her and then she's gonna be like 'cool sorry I was just wanting sex only and you misunderstood everything' and then she won't want to talk to me ever again and the band will fall apart and everything will suck forever."

In the wake of my terrified rant, my bandmates were silent. And then Simon sat up and looked at me. "She's not Eva, Felix," he said quietly.

To my horror, tears stung my eyes. "I know," I managed, swiping angrily at my cheeks. "I just…"

"What if she says yes?" Wendy asked from his spot on the ground. "Like, purely hypothetically, what if she feels the same way?"

The thought made me feel like balloons were

expanding inside my chest. "If Rose wanted to be with me," I said. "I would…Jesus damn, I would be scared out of my mind and also the happiest I've ever been."

"You gotta tell her, then!" Aaron exclaimed.

I took a deep breath. "If it goes to shit, am I allowed to have like, a total breakdown?"

Simon smiled. "Complete and total breakdown allowed." he said. "I don't even know what that would look like for you, honestly, but we're here for you."

"We gotta make a plan," Wendy said. All four of us were sitting up now. "Otherwise you'll just pine and nothing will happen. Have her come over tomorrow."

"*Tomorrow?*" I exclaimed, eyebrows raised. "Jesus, give a guy some time to prepare!"

"That's at least fifteen hours to prepare," Wendy shrugged. He reached over to the chair where I'd been sitting and grabbed my phone. "Besides, what do you even need to prepare? Text her right now and tell her to come over tomorrow."

I took my phone from Wendy with shaking hands. And when I unlocked it, I saw that Rose had already sent me a text.

> ROSE: Hey, can I talk to you tomorrow
> night sometime?

Equal parts dread and relief filled me.

> ME: Come over at 7

CHAPTER 32

All I Had To Do

ROSE

I didn't think I'd ever felt more terrified in my life. I had just raised my hand to knock on Felix's door when it swung open. He stood there for a moment, looking at me.

He looked so handsome. His sharp features and green eyes, lined in black. His expression was guarded, but still, for a moment, I forgot how to breathe.

"Hey," Felix said. "Come on in."

I nodded, then followed him on shaking legs until we got to his bedroom. The rest of the house was empty. He shut the door, then sat on the edge of his bed.

"Want to sit down?" Felix asked, patting the spot next to him.

Honestly, I didn't think I could survive being any closer to Felix. "I'm okay." I pulled the piece of paper out of my pocket, the one where I'd written an outline for what I wanted to say.

"Are you sure?" Felix asked, his eyes darting to the paper I was holding. "We could—"

I held up a hand. "Just…don't…say anything for a minute," I stammered. "I need to say this and if you say something before I'm done I'll never say it."

Felix nodded without smiling.

I glance down at the slip of paper in my hand. "When we were seniors in high school," I said, "All I wanted was to dance with you at prom." I looked up to see Felix's mouth fall open in surprise.

"I watched you from across the greenhouse," I continued. "Dancing with Xalia while 'At Last' played over the sound system, and I wished it was me."

My voice was shaking. So were my hands. My heart felt like it was going to explode out of my chest, and suddenly I didn't know if I could do this. Felix was watching me so intently and I felt more naked now than I ever did when we were having sex. But I had to tell him. I would probably die if I didn't.

"I think about that night a lot," I continued. "I think about how all I had to do was ask you to dance. Like, maybe the only reason you didn't dance with me that night was because I never said anything to you about it. It still —" I swallowed to steady my voice. "It still breaks my heart that I never got to have that with you."

The familiar ache I'd felt about Felix for so many years was pooling in my chest, the despair of loving him that I'd come to know so well. It almost stopped my words. The outline I held in one hand was suddenly useless, and I crumpled it into my pocket. I took another shaky breath, then looked down at the floor. I wouldn't be able to finish if I was looking at him.

"I've loved you for a long time, Felix," I whispered. My words came out in a halting, stumbling rush. "I've…I've been in love with you since we were sixteen. I should have told you a long time ago, and I really should have told you back when you first offered to kiss me. I feel awful that you did all that without knowing how I really feel. But I'm telling you now. Because if I had told you that I wanted to dance with you at prom, maybe I could have had that. And I have no idea what's going to happen or how you feel, but I had to tell you that I…I'm in love with you. Otherwise I'll regret it for the rest of my life. So I had to say it out loud to you, at least once."

The room was silent for a full twenty seconds. It was twenty seconds of agony before I finally managed to lift my eyes. Felix was looking at me with such intense emotion—I had never seen him look like that. It was fear and sorrow and shock and something else I couldn't identify. My heart stuttered.

"Felix?" I said.

And then Felix covered his face with his hands and burst into tears.

I stood frozen, with no idea what his response could mean. The only other time I'd seen him cry was when he broke up with Eva. But I wasn't breaking up with him, I was—

"Rose," he said through his tears.

Without even thinking, I stepped toward him, closing the distance between us. And then Felix collapsed onto his knees and wrapped his arms around my waist, burying his face in my stomach.

I didn't know what any of it meant. I reached up and hesitantly ran a hand through his hair, and it made Felix squeeze me so tightly that it seemed to crush my bones. When he spoke, his words were muffled against my body.

"I'm in love with you," he said.

I froze. I couldn't have heard him right. "What?" I gasped.

Felix tilted his face to look up at me, his chin resting on my stomach. "I'm in love with you."

The world stopped. Stars were exploding behind my heart. There were fireworks in my blood, and every single one of my cells was singing with light and music and laughter and every good thing the world had ever known.

"Are you sure?" I asked.

Felix smiled at me, tears shining in his eyes. "Yes, I'm sure, Rose."

I gazed down into the face of the boy I'd loved for almost a decade, trying to orient myself to this new reality, one in which Felix loved me the way I'd loved him for so long. "What about…?" I started.

But I didn't know how to finish my question. I didn't even know what my question was. Felix looked into my eyes and spoke softly. "Rose, I am scared out of my fucking mind about this. I'm scared about losing everything—the band, the friendships we have. My friendship with you. But something happened in the past few months and I…I just can't imagine my life without you in my arms. I think it's always been you."

I fell to my knees in front of him, gripping his shirt in my fists. "Say it again," I whispered.

"Which part?"

"About being in love with me." I could hear the desperation in my voice.

Felix took my face in his hands, his green eyes looking deeply into mine. "I'm in love with you."

This time it was my turn to burst into tears. But Felix pressed his lips to my cheek and whispered, "I'm in love with you." His mouth moved from my cheeks to my jaw to my eyelids, each time softly repeating the phrase, "I'm in love with you, I'm in love with you, I'm in love with you." When he finally pressed his lips to mine, I could taste the salt of my tears mingling with his. We pulled apart and I whispered, "I love you."

And then Felix's lips were on mine again, hungry this time. His hand cupped the back of my head, deepening our kiss. When I parted my lips, he made a hungry sound deep in his throat, and his other arm wrapped around my back and pulled me closer to him.

I was falling into him, melting, desperate to have his skin on mine.

My hands found the hem of his shirt and pulled it over his head, and he did the same with my shirt. It was fumbling and joyful, both of us half laughing, half crying as we pulled each other's clothes off.

His bed was right there next to us, but I couldn't imagine one second of our bodies being parted long enough for us to climb into it. I stretched my body out on the carpet, pulling Felix down over me, kissing him with everything in me. I ran my hands up and down his bare arms, splayed my fingers over his chest, reached up to touch his jaw.

It was different now. It was different because he knew. Because I was allowed to show him all of the love I'd been carrying for so long and somehow, against all odds, after all this time, he was in love with me, too.

Felix was hard against my stomach, his hips tilting, seeking even deeper connection. It was agony when he rose to kneel long enough to roll on a condom.

When he pushed himself inside of me, my eyes stung with another wave of tears, and I heard myself cry out softly.

Felix froze, then gazed down at me. "Are you okay?" he gasped.

I looked up into his face. "I'm happy," I said through

my tears. I reached up to cup his jaw. "I'm just really, really happy."

"Shit fuck, Rose, I love you," Felix replied. He kept his eyes locked on mine while he drew his hips back and then pushed into me again, filling me perfectly.

It was almost too much. Too much pleasure, too much joy, too much love. All I could do was cling to Felix as our bodies moved together, as we let touch and breath say everything that words couldn't say. Later, there would be time for talking. Right now, Felix was kissing me like he knew me, like I was the only thing in the world that mattered, and it was all I needed.

CHAPTER 33
At Last

FELIX

Nothing had ever felt as right or as perfect as being with Rose like this. I was drowning in the heat of her, clutching at the softness and sweetness that made up her whole self. It seemed unreal—that this kind and beautiful and incredible woman, the one currently gasping my name in pleasure, was in love with me.

I was in love with Rose, and she was in love with me. My lips pressed to a spot on Rose's neck as I moved inside her. I could feel her breath growing faster, her fingers gripping me more tightly, so I reached down between our bodies and moved my fingers in the way I remembered her showing me—bigger and smaller circles, until she was clenching around me, coming apart beneath me. And then I was unraveling, too, absolutely falling to pieces, hissing out Rose's name as I poured everything I felt for her into this moment.

As our breath slowed, I looked down into her face, her brown eyes gazing up at me, her lips full and perfect. Rose loved me. *Rose was in love with me.* After every shitty non-relationship I'd ever had, after Kendra and Eva and everyone I ever denied yearning for, the perfect girl had been right here for me all along. I loved Rose more than I knew was possible. It was overwhelming, all this love. I felt tears prick my eyes and I sat up, covering my face with one hand.

"Felix," Rose whispered, her voice tender.

I leaned against my bed and dropped my hand to look at her. "Goddamn I'm in love with you, Rose."

Rose's teary smile was blinding. She crawled into my lap, facing me, her legs wrapped around me, and we held each other and cried and kissed until we were laughing.

Finally, after I had taken care of the condom, I pulled us into my bed, and Rose settled herself into my side, her head on my chest. I gazed up at the ceiling, drowsy with emotion.

"This is actually insane," I said quietly.

"Which part?" Rose asked.

I found myself chuckling. "Jesus, all of it. The fact that I'm in love with you and you're in love with me, that all of this started with a friendship when we were sixteen, that you're naked in my bed right now."

"If you think this is insane, imagine how I feel," Rose replied, a smile in her voice. "I've been thinking about this for like, eight years."

My fingers drifted gently up and down Rose's back. "Was it really that long?"

Rose looked up at me and nodded. "I'm sorry I didn't tell you sooner," she said.

I brushed some of her hair away from her face. "I understand why you didn't. But I'm glad you told me today."

Rose hesitated for a moment before asking, "Does it

change how you feel about us kissing and having sex before this?"

My gaze went back to the ceiling. *Did* it change how I felt? "Honestly…" I started. "Honestly, no. Like, I get that maybe I'm supposed to feel deceived or something, but I'm just too happy that you feel the same way about me to care. And you were handling it way more maturely than I would have if I were in your position."

"Can I ask you another question?" Rose said.

"Yeah."

"Why did you offer to kiss me? Back when you first found out about me not having my first kiss?"

I stared at the ceiling. "I don't even know if I can answer that," I replied. "I offered because I wanted you to have a good first experience, and I cared about you. I probably loved you even then. If not fully, then like, the seeds were there. The potential for being in love with you was at the tipping point of spilling over into actually being in love with you. Something in my soul answered the call. Or something."

Rose squeezed me tightly and then left a trail of kisses over my chest. My eyes fell closed. She was so fucking sweet it made my jaw clench with affection. I would get to have this all the time. Rose, in my arms, in my bed and at shows and…

Shit. Shows. We were in a band together. Shit.

"Hey, Rose?" I asked.

"Hmmm?" she whispered between kisses.

Ugh, her voice was soft and sultry and my dick was already responding again, but this was important. I sat up and looked at her. "Did you talk to the rest of Queen Anne about this?"

Rose gazed at me, then sat up and nodded.

"And they're okay if we're together?" I asked. "We're already bending the Oregon Rule for Marlowe and Simon and—"

Rose stopped me with a kiss. When we pulled apart, she leaned her forehead on mine. "They were the ones who convinced me to tell you," she said.

"Smart women," I murmured.

"What about the boys?" Rose asked, pulling away to look at me.

"They're also on team Felix and Rose," I replied.

Rose smiled at me and reached down to wrap her hand around my cock. She gave me a gentle squeeze and my eyes practically rolled into the back of my head.

"So what I'm hearing," she whispered, "is that we get to be together. And do all of this all the time."

I was already hard and getting harder, and I reached back to steady myself with one hand while she worked me. God, for someone with very little experience, she was really good at this.

Wait. A terrible realization was swirling in my stomach. I frowned, then opened my eyes.

"Rose," I said, grabbing one of her wrists.

"Yes?" she asked, looking innocent. Shit, who knew she could tease like this?

"Hang on, I feel…"

She reached out with her other hand and gave another slow stroke of my dick. "You feel…?"

"This…isn't…fair," I managed.

"Which part?"

If she kept going, I wasn't going to be able to goddamn think, and forget talking. "Wait, actually hang on for a second," I said, pushing her hands away. "It's not fair that…shit fuck, that I'm the only one you've ever had sex with. Like, there are other things…to do that you haven't done yet. Other people you could be with."

"*You* can show me things," she said, smiling coyly and leaning in.

I grabbed her shoulders. I couldn't believe I was about to say this, but I wanted her to have whatever she needed. "I mean it, Rose. If ever you want like, a hall pass or something…" I swallowed, because I felt like I was literally going to die at the thought, but I didn't want to stop Rose from having the experiences she wanted.

Rose's teasing smile melted away, leaving tenderness in its place. "Thank you," she said. "But…Felix, you're it for me. You always have been."

Her words ricocheted through me, leaving me feeling golden and glowing.

"Are you sure?" I asked. I didn't know what the hell I was saying. It was probably some stupid attempt at self-sabotage, but apparently Rose wasn't going to let me get away with it.

"I'm sure," Rose said. Her voice matched her words. "If ever I change my mind, I'll tell you. But I'm sure."

I nodded. Truly, the idea of Rose having sex with anyone else was going to send me into an actual mental breakdown, so I reached out and held her face in my hands.

"I fucking love you," I said.

"I fucking love you," she replied. I saw something pass over her face, some uncertainty. "But, um…"

Dread curled in my stomach and I dropped my hands, but Rose reached out and held them again. "No! Don't look like that! I love you. I just wanted to say one more thing."

"Okay, hurry, because this is a lot of feelings for me in one night."

Rose gazed at the bedspread. "I meant what I said to you at the show, about standing up for myself. I've given a lot over the years, to you, I mean. When you and Eva…"

My eyes shut. That must have been torture. Hell, it was torture for me, but when I thought back to the way I had cried to Rose about it, I could only imagine how much it broke her heart.

"Rose, I'm sorry," I said.

"It's okay," she replied. "I would do it again. And I want to still be there for you, even in hard times. But I also don't want to tear myself to pieces for anyone. Even you." She looked up at me, still looking uncertain.

Relief and love ballooned in my chest. "Rose," I said. "I would never forgive myself if you tore yourself to pieces for me. Or anyone."

"It might take me some practice for me to avoid it," she replied.

I grinned at her. "We both know I'm happy to help you practice with anything you want."

Rose returned my grin. "After all these years, Felix Christopolous is my boyfriend."

I leaned in and kissed her softly. "Was it worth it? All that waiting?"

"I would have waited another eight years," Rose replied. My heart stuttered as I looked into her brown eyes. "But I'm glad I don't have to."

Rose kissed me again, pushing me down onto the bed. My arms came up around her and this time, it was slower. We lingered, touching, exploring, knowing we had all the time in the world. And when it was over, after we had both collapsed in pleasure again, I took Rose's face in my hands and kissed her gently.

"I'm glad it was you," Rose whispered against my lips. "For my first kiss. My first everything."

I leaned my forehead to hers. "I don't know if anyone else in the world could have convinced me that romance was for me after all."

"I'm glad I could be your first, too, then," Rose replied. Then I pressed my lips to hers. Again and again and again.

CHAPTER 34

"Her Kisses"

TWO WEEKS LATER

ROSE

"This song is a new one!" Simon said into the mic. He threw a glance over his shoulder to Felix, then over to me. "None of us got into music to find romance, even though I now have a super hot rock star girlfriend. But before we play this song, I would like to announce that Felix and Rose here finally got together, after being friends for like, a million years." The crowd cheered, and I found myself grinning.

"Eight years!" Felix hollered.

"Right, eight years," Simon said. "So now there are two couples in Queenscout, so if you hate love, leave before we play this next song."

"Just for clarification," Jem said into her mic, "No one else from this band is getting together." She turned and glared at Wendy, Ducky, and Aaron, who all laughed.

Aaron stepped up to Jem's mic. "The rest of us will find our love stories outside of this band," he said.

Then Felix laid his fingers over his keyboard and

played the intro to "Her Kisses," which we'd just learned last week. The lyrics were vague enough to be about anyone, but all of us knew that Felix had written it for me. I was nervous to play it in front of an audience. It felt vulnerable in a way that playing other songs didn't.

But then I caught Felix's eye and everything else fell away. His black eyeliner was thicker than usual for the show, but his green eyes locked onto mine and I was anchored in place. The venue could crumble around us, and I would still be here, looking at Felix across the stage while we played a song with our band.

There were moments when it almost didn't seem real to me—having Felix, being with him. How many times had I dreamt of this exact thing? Playing in a band together after kissing briefly backstage?

Our being together had softened Felix a little bit. He was still gruff and standoffish with most people, and definitely with strangers. But his smile was much closer to the surface nowadays. And I was learning that apparently Felix was a very cuddly boyfriend. He was always reaching for my hand, wrapping an arm around my waist, resting his chin on my head. The last time I went over to the boys' house, he had pulled me into his lap and kept me there for two hours, nudging his nose along my arm now and then. It made my bones sing with happiness. All this friendship. All this love.

"You guys go, we'll catch up with you," Felix said, his voice echoing in the now empty venue. Almost everyone else had loaded up their gear, and Felix and I were just finishing packing our stuff.

"Fine," Ducky said, turning to leave. "Don't have sex in here," she admonished over her shoulder.

"Ducky!" I exclaimed. Jem swatted her arm.

"This is literally about hygiene!" she replied.

My stomach clenched uncomfortably at her teasing. I spent a moment debating with myself, and then I raised my eyes and said, "Hey, Ducky? Could you not make jokes about my sex life? Please?"

Ducky looked into my eyes and then her face fell. "Sorry, hon," she said. "I didn't realize it bothered you."

"Thanks," I replied. "We're good, I just don't like it so I thought I'd say something."

Ducky dropped her bag of drumsticks and strode toward me. "I love you for saying something," she said, her arms wrapping around me. "Always say something."

"You got it," I said, hugging her back. Over Marlowe's shoulder, Jem smiled at me, and I smiled back.

And then it was just Felix and me. I turned to see him looking at me, his hands shoved into his pockets. His tongue worried his lip ring, the way he always did when he was thinking hard about something.

"Is everything okay?" I asked.

"Yeah," he said. Then he turned and wordlessly walked back to the tech booth. After a moment, the room was plunged into total darkness. Then Felix hit a switch that illuminated the disco ball in the middle of the venue, sending sparkling dots of light across the walls and floor. Then he hit another button on the sound board. When I heard the first few notes of the song playing, my heart stuttered in my chest and my eyes flew to Felix's.

I watched him walk toward me, Etta James' voice singing out that aching first "At Last." Felix stopped in front of me and held out his hand. "Dance with me?" he said.

My whole body filled with warmth. It felt like my heart was smiling, like I was melting into a lake of sweetness. This boy. This perfect, wonderful, deeply caring boy. I reached out and clasped Felix's hand, then stepped into him.

He wrapped an arm around my waist and pulled me into him. He rested his head against my temple, and my eyes fluttered closed. We swayed in a slow circle, listening to the desperately romantic music.

"I know it's not the same," Felix whispered.

I nestled my face into his shoulder for a moment, then placed a kiss on his chest. "It's better," I replied.

Felix let go of my waist to bring his hand to my chin, tilting my face up toward him. His green eyes moved over my features, taking me in. He did this a lot these days—just looked at me. I let myself look back. I didn't have to guard my expression or try not to stare for too long now. I didn't think I would ever get tired of being able to just look at him like this. I reached up to trace a finger over one of his eyebrows, down his sharp nose, then over his lip. His mouth fell open at my touch, then he leaned down and kissed me.

"You're right," he whispered. "We probably wouldn't have kissed at prom."

"I would have *fainted* if we had kissed at prom," I replied.

Felix chuckled. "I remember thinking that you looked really pretty that night. With your short hair and your long, red dress."

I stared up at him. "You remember that dress?"

Felix looked thoughtfully into the distance. "I probably loved you then and just didn't know it. Because I'm a fucking idiot."

"You're not a fucking idiot," I said.

"Wanna know when I actually fell in love with you?" Felix asked, returning his gaze to mine. "For sure?"

"Yes," I breathed.

"The night we listened to the Stonewallflower album," he said. "When I kissed you that night, it was because I wanted to."

My pulse thudded in my veins. "That night felt different to me, too," I told him quietly. Then I smiled up into his face. "I fell in love with you the night we fixed Xalia's mic in the middle of a show."

Felix's eyebrows knitted together. "Did you say something to me about getting taller that night?"

I nodded.

Felix took our joined hands and pressed them to his chest. "I was so shitting dumb," he said.

"I was in love with you anyway," I said. "I kept thinking that phrase over and over again for the rest of that night. 'I'm in love with him, I'm in love with him, I'm in love with him...'"

Felix stopped dancing and took my face in his hands. "I'm in love with you," he whispered. His eyes looked deep into mine, and then he leaned forward and kissed me. His soft lips moved gently, tasting, teasing.

I would never ever get tired of kissing Felix. I thought about pulling away to tell him so, but for now, I just let my kisses speak for me.

A Longing Time
By Rose Devangelo

Some people wait
For a flash of light
To tell them what their heart knows.
Some spot of illumination.
Last night we danced among thousands of them.
You're here now. I'm here.
All the walls between us broken down
by every memory of when you've undone me.
I had grown so used
to longing that I forgot that love
could feel light.

Acknowledgments

I will never be able to express enough gratitude to the readers who pick up my books. Thank you for making this little daydreamy novelist's daydreams come true.

Thank you for the beta readers who helped refine this story: Elliott Croft, Sam Baird, Ashley Coombs, Lindsay Marriott, Sara Goldberg-McRae, Andy Hansen (special thanks for the note about "Chekhov's Vibrator"), and fellow indie author EJ Hopps (check out her Chef's Kiss series on Kindle Unlimited and Amazon!)

Thanks to Ellie Otis for being my #1 proofreader and hype woman.

Special thanks to Carleigh and Sara for problem-solving first-time hand job scenes. And thanks to Lucas Stewart for helping me figure out sexy alternate ways to clarify that the characters mean intercourse.

Thanks always to the Salt Lake/Provo music scene & the Deep Love family.

Special thanks to the Bollywood film *Kuch Kuch Hota Hai* for being the OG "friends to lovers, carrying a torch forever, last to know" romance of my heart.

Love to Chase and Lillian, the best housemates I could ask for, my favorite example of friends to lovers, and the reason there are now *Twilight* references in all of my books.

Shout out to Mrs. Tadema, the best high school drama teacher ever.

I am always indebted to the Facebook groups The Writing Gals, 20BooksTo50K, Self Publishing Support

Group, and Romance Writers Support League, as well as Kindlepreneur.

I express my love and gratitude to Jesse and Kathleen, whose long friendship and eventual romance have long shaped my understanding of love. (I think of you and miss you often, Kathleeny.)

My love to Oma, whose love story with Opa is another lesson in love, and whose financial support makes my work possible.

And finally, love to every boy and girl I've ever yearned for. Moments when my heart broke and moments when my heart flew because of you have made me love romance even more deeply, and shaped this story more than any other I've written so far.

Also by Elle Whittaker

WEST TINDALE

Halfway to You (August 2025)

Halfway Across the Street (September 2025)

Halfway Through the Holidays (December 2024)

ROCK ROMANCE

Rules Worth Breaking (July 2025)

ENCOUNTERS

Under His Hands

At Your Service

OTHER THINGS

Jane Eyre and Zombies

About the Author

Elle Whittaker is the pen name for Liz Whittaker, who is the daughter of a poem and an ancient Egyptian hieroglyph. She spent most of her time on the shores of Neverland before moving to Salt Lake City, where she currently lives in a library until she can afford an RV. Her heart alternates between pumping lemonade and ink. Her favorite foods are music and knowledge, which she eats as often as possible from atop her mountain of crippling student debt. Her other job is theatre/film. In her free time, she enjoys hugging trees, completing jigsaw puzzles, and thinking about outer space. She is happily a victim of the kind of moonstruck madness that drives her to not only write romance novels, but poetry, scripts, essays, and theatre reviews under various names.

instagram.com/ellewhittakerromance

tiktok.com/@elle.whittaker.romance